ABERDEEN
CITY LIBRARIES
www.aberdeencity.gov.uk/libraries

Return to...
or any other Aberdeen City Library

Please return/renew this item by the last date shown
Items may also be renewed by phone or online

He'd tried to block out the intense need that had been rioting through him from the moment he'd gotten out of bed last night and left her there alone when he'd wanted nothing more than to take her again. And again. And again.

Dante wanted even more to try and eradicate the pain in his chest that seemed to hit him so hard and strong whenever he looked at Paige holding Ana. A mother and her child. The love that passed between them. The truest love he'd known. The love he had lost.

He wanted to crush those feelings. Bury them beneath something stronger. Lust. Sex. Desire.

"Don't ignore me, Paige," he said. He swept her hair to the side and bent, pressing a kiss to the side of her neck. "Ever."

She shivered beneath his touch. "I wasn't."

"You were trying to ignore this." He traced the line of her neck with the tip of his tongue. "And you know we can't."

Maisey Yates was an avid Mills & Boon® Modern™ Romance reader before she began to write them. She still can't quite believe she's lucky enough to get to create her very own sexy alpha heroes and feisty heroines. Seeing her name on one of those lovely covers is a dream come true.

Maisey lives with her handsome, wonderful, diaper-changing husband and three small children across the street from her extremely supportive parents and the home she grew up in, in the wilds of Southern Oregon, USA. She enjoys the contrast of living in a place where you might wake up to find a bear on your back porch and then heading into the home office to write stories that take place in exotic urban locales.

Recent titles by the same author:

AT HIS MAJESTY'S COMMAND*
A GAME OF VOWS
A ROYAL WORLD APART*
ONE NIGHT IN PARADISE *(One Night In...)*

**linked duet*

HER LITTLE WHITE LIE

BY
MAISEY YATES

First published in Great Britain 2013
by Mills & Boon, an imprint of Harlequin (UK) Limited.
Harlequin (UK) Limited, Eton House, 18-24 Paradise Road,
Richmond, Surrey TW9 1SR

© Maisey Yates 2013

ISBN: 978 0 263 23393 3

Harlequin (UK) policy is to use papers that are natural, renewable
and recyclable products and made from wood grown in sustainable
forests. The logging and manufacturing process conform to the
legal environmental regulations of the country of origin.

Printed and bound in Great Britain
by CPI Antony Rowe, Chippenham, Wiltshire

B000 000 008 1224

HER LITTLE
WHITE LIE

For my grandma,
who passed on her love of books and romance to me.

CHAPTER ONE

"EXPLAIN this, or pack up your things and get out."

Paige Harper looked up from her seated position and into her boss's dark, angry eyes. Having him here, in her office, was enough to leave her speechless. Breathless. He was handsome from far away and, up close, even enraged, he was arresting. It was hard to look away from him, but she managed. Then she looked down at the newspaper he'd thrown onto the surface of her desk and her heart sank into her stomach.

"Oh…" She picked up the paper. "Oh…"

"Speechless?"

"Oh…"

"I said explain, Ms. Harper. 'Oh' is not an explanation in any language that I am aware of." He crossed his arms over his broad chest and Paige suddenly felt two inches tall.

"I…" She looked back down at the paper, open to the lifestyle section, the main headline reading Dante Romani to Tie the Knot with Employee. Underneath the headline were two pictures. One of Dante, looking forbidding and perfectly pressed in a custom-made suit. And one of her, on a ladder, in a window at Colson's, hanging strips of tinsel from the ceiling in preparation for the holiday season.

"I…" She tried again as she scanned the article.

Dante Romani, notorious bad boy of the Colson Department Store empire, who just last week made headlines for the callous axing of a top exec, and for replacing the family man in favor of a younger, less-attached man, is now engaged to one of his employees. We can't help but wonder if playing games with his staff is a favored pastime of the much-maligned businessman. Either firing them or marrying them at will.

Her stomach tightened with horror. She couldn't fathom how this had ended up in the paper. She'd done a fair amount of panicking over how she was going to fix the lie she'd told the social worker, but she'd thought she would have some time. She hadn't expected this, not even in her wildest dreams.

But there it was, the lie of the century, shouting at her in black and white.

"That's hardly more eloquent, or more informative."

"I told a lie," she said.

He looked around her office, and her eyes followed his, over the stacks of fabric samples, boxes with beads hanging out of them, aerosol cans of flocking and paint sitting in the corner and Christmas knickknacks spread over every surface.

He looked back at her, his lip curled upward. "On second thought, why don't you skip packing and just walk out. I can have your things express delivered to you."

"Wait...no..." Losing her job was unthinkable, as was getting caught in her lie. She needed her job. And she really didn't need child services to find out she'd lied during her adoption interview. Well, what she really needed was a time machine so that she could go back and opt not to lie to Rebecca Addler, but that was probably a bit too complicated as solutions went.

She looked back down at the article.

It's hard to imagine that a man who so recently fired someone for being, reportedly more devoted to his family than to the almighty dollar, could settle down and become a family man himself. The question is: Can this thoroughly average woman reform the soulless CEO? Or will she become another in the long line of professional and personal casualties Dante Romani leaves in his wake?

Average woman. Yeah, that sounded like her life. Even in her lie, where she was engaged to the hottest billionaire in town, she came out of it as the average woman.

She swallowed and looked back up at her boss's blazing expression. "This is horrible journalism. Sensationalist nonsense, really. All but an opinion piece, one might say. Fluff, even."

Dante cut her off, his black eyes hard, flat. "What did you hope to accomplish with this? Was it fun gossip you didn't think would spread around to this degree? Or was it something you wanted?"

She stood, her knees shaking. "No, I just…"

"You might not be newsworthy, Ms. Harper, but I am."

"Hey!" The assessment burned, especially on the heels of the descriptor of her as "average." Of course, she had to admit, looking at their pictures side by side, that *average* was a pretty kind descriptor.

"Did I offend you?"

"A little."

"I guarantee it is not half so offensive as coming into work to discover you're engaged to someone you have barely had four conversations with."

"Actually, I'm sort of in the same boat you are. I didn't expect for this to be in the paper. I didn't…I didn't expect for anyone to ever find out."

"Be that as it may, they have. And now I have. It would be best if you were to see yourself out. I do not wish to call security." He turned and started to walk out of the room and she felt her heart slide the rest of the way down.

"Mr. Romani," she said, "please, hear me out." She was nearly pleading. No, who was she kidding? She *was* pleading. And she wasn't ashamed. She would get down on her knees and beg if she had to, but she wasn't going to let him ruin this.

"I tried. You had nothing of interest to say."

"Because I don't know where to start."

"The beginning works for me."

She took a deep breath. "Rebecca Addler frowns on single mothers. Not every social worker does, but this one...this one doesn't like them. I mean, not that she doesn't like them personally, but in general. And she asked me why Ana would be better off with me as opposed to a real, traditional family with a mother and a father and I just sort of told her that there would be a father because I was getting married and then your name slipped out because...well, because I work for you, so I see it a lot and it was the first name I thought of."

He blinked twice, then shifted, his head tilted to the side. "That was not the beginning."

Paige took another deep breath, trying to slow down her brain and find a better starting point. "I'm trying to adopt."

He frowned. "I didn't know."

"Well, I have my daughter in the day care here."

"I don't go to the day care," he said, his tone flat.

"Ana's just a baby. She's been with me almost from the moment she was born. I..." Thinking of Shyla still made her throat tighten, made her ache everywhere. Her beautiful, vivacious best friend. The only person who'd really enjoyed her eccentricity rather than simply bearing it. "Her mother is gone. And I'm taking care of her. Nothing was made official before Shyla...anyway she's a ward now."

"Meaning?"

"Meaning the state has the final say over her placement. It's been fine for me to foster her, I'm approved for that. But... but not necessarily for adopting. I've been trying and I had a meeting with the worker handling the case two days ago. It was looking like they weren't going to approve the adoption.

And yes, I lied. About us. And about…the engagement, but please believe it had nothing to do with you."

A slight lie. It had a lot to do with the fact that he was much better looking than any man had a right to be. And she had to go in to work in the same building as he did, and chance walking by him in the halls. Being exposed to all that male beauty was a hazard.

So, yes, there were times she thought of him away from work. In fairness, he was the best-looking man she'd ever encountered in her entire life, and she was in a dating dry spell of epic proportions, which meant, pleasant time with images of Dante was about all she had going on in her love life.

And she saw the man all the time, and that made things worse.

As a result of the exposure, when pressed for the name of her fiancé by Rebecca Addler, the only man she'd been able to picture had been Dante. And so his name had sort of spilled out.

Another gaffe in a long line of them for her. When it came to "oops," she was well above average.

So there, newspaper reporter.

One of his dark eyebrows shot upward. "I'm flattered."

She put her hand on her forehead. "There is no way for me to win trying to explain this," she said. "It's just awkward. But…but…I don't really know what to do now. It wasn't supposed to be in the paper, and now it is, and if it turns out we aren't engaged they'll know that I lied and then…"

"And then you'll be a single mother who is also a liar. Two strikes, I would think." His tone was so disengaged, so unfeeling.

She swallowed. "Well, exactly."

He was right. Two strikes. If not a plain old strikeout. It wasn't an acceptable risk. Not where Ana was concerned. Ana, the brightest spot in her life. Her helpless little girl, the baby she loved more than her own life. There was nothing and no one else she would even consider stooping to this level of subterfuge for, nothing else that could possibly compel her to do what she was starting to think she had to do: propose to her boss.

The man who practically stole the air from her lungs when he walked into a room. The man who was so far out of her league, even thinking of a dinner date with him was laughable.

But this was bigger than that. Bigger than a little crush or her insecurity. Her fear of outright rejection.

"I...I think I need your help."

There was no change in his expression. Dante Romani was impossible to read, but then, that wasn't really new. He was the dark prince of the Colson empire, the adopted son of Don and Mary Colson. The media speculated that they'd adopted him because he'd shown profound brilliance at an early age. No one imagined it had been his personality that had won over the older couple.

She'd always thought those stories were sad and unfair. Now she wondered. Wondered if he was as heartless as he was portrayed to be. She really hoped he wasn't, because she was going to need him to care at least a little bit in order to pull this off.

"I'm not in the position to give this kind of help," he said, his tone dry.

"Why?" she asked, pushing herself into a standing position. "Why not? I...I don't need you forever, I just need..."

"You need me to marry you. I think that's a step too far into crazy town, don't you?"

"For my daughter," she said, the words raw, loud and echoing in the room. And now that she'd said them, out loud, she didn't regret them. She would do anything for Ana. Even this. Even if it meant getting thrown out of the office building.

Because for the first time in her memory, something mattered. It mattered more than self-protection or fending off disappointment. It was worth the possibility of adding to her list of failures.

"She's not your daughter," he said.

She gritted her teeth, trying to keep a handle on the adrenaline that was pounding through her, making her shake. "Blood isn't everything. I would think you would understand that." Probably not the best idea to be taking shots at him, but it was true. He should understand.

He regarded her for a moment, a muscle ticking in his jaw. "I will not fire you. For now. But I will require further explanation. An explanation that makes sense. What do you have on your agenda for the day?"

"I'm working on Christmas," she said, indicating the array of decorations spread out in the room. "For Colson's and for Trinka." She was working on a series of elegant displays for the parent store, and for their offshoot, teen clothing store, something mod and edgy.

"You'll be in the office?"

She nodded. "Just fiddling today."

"Good. Don't leave until we've spoken again." He turned and walked out of her office and she sank to her knees, her hands shaking, her entire body wound so tight she wanted to curl in on herself.

She was so stupid. Nothing new. She'd spoken without thinking. As per usual. Only this time it had landed her in serious trouble, with the man who signed her checks.

Everything was in his hands now. Her future. Her family. Her money.

"Time to learn to think before you talk," she said into the empty office. Unfortunately, it was too late for that. Way, way too late.

Dante finished with the last item of work on his agenda and turned to his file cabinet, placing the last document on his desk into its appropriate spot. Then he put his elbows on the desk and leaned forward, staring at the newspaper on the shining surface.

He'd studied the news story again when he'd come back

into his office. A scathing piece on how the impostor of the Colson family moved people around like pawns on a chessboard. It was stacked with details about the man, Carl Johnson, he'd fired last week for skipping out on an important meeting to go to a child's sporting event.

The press had covered it a week ago, too, since Carl had gone screaming to the papers over discrimination of some kind. In Dante's mind, it wasn't discrimination to expect an employee to attend mandatory meetings, no matter whether it was the last game of a five-year-old's T-ball season or not.

Still, it had been another of those juicy bits the media had latched on to to further stack the case against him and his possession of human decency. It generally didn't matter to him.

But one thing in that article stood out to him: Can she reform him?

Could Paige Harper reform him? The idea amused him. He had the bare minimum of contact with her. She did her job, and she did it well, so he never had a reason to involve himself. But he had noticed her. Impossible not to. She was a blur of shimmer when she moved around the office. Boundless energy and a sense of the accidental radiated from her.

He would be lying if he said he wasn't intrigued by her. She was a window into so many things he would never seek out: chaos, color, motion. So many things he would never be. Combined with the fact that she had a figure most men would be hard-pressed to ignore, and yes, he was intrigued by her.

But no matter how intrigued, she simply wasn't the sort of woman he would normally approach. Until this.

"Can this thoroughly average woman reform the soulless CEO?"

He had no desire to take part in a reformation, but the idea of an image overhaul in the media? That had possibilities.

He could have demanded a retraction the moment he'd walked in that morning. Or he could let it run. Let them build off the image they'd created for him when he'd been thrust into the spotlight. A fourteen-year-old boy, adopted, finally, and suspected of being capable of all manner of violence and sociopathic behaviors.

His story had been written in the public eye before he'd had a chance to live it. And so he had never challenged it. Had never cared.

But suddenly he had been handed a tool that might help change things.

He turned around and faced the windows, looked out at the harbor. He could still see the look on her face. Not just the expression, but the depth of fear and desperation in her eyes. The press had a few things right about him, and one of them was that feelings, emotions, mattered little to him. And still…still he couldn't forget. And he thought of the baby, too.

He had no use for children. No desire for them. But he could remember being one all too well. Could remember being passed around the foster care system for eight years of his life. Could remember what it was like to be at the mercy of either the State, or, before that, adults who brought harm, not love.

Could he consign Ana to that same fate? Or to a family who might not feel that same desperate longing that Paige seemed to feel for her?

And why should he care at all? That was the million-dollar question. Caring wasn't counted among his usual afflictions.

The door to his office opened and Paige breezed in. Maybe breezed was the wrong term. A breeze denoted something gentle, soothing even. Paige was more a gale-force wind.

She had a big, gold bag hanging off her shoulder, one that matched her glittering, golden pumps that likely added four inches to her height. She also had a bolt of fabric held tightly beneath the other arm, and a large sketchbook beneath that. She looked like she might drop all of it at any moment.

She plunked her things down in the chair in front of his desk, bending at the waist, her skirt tightening over the curve of her butt, and pushed her hand back through her dark brown hair, revealing a streak of bright pink nearly hidden beneath the top layers.

She was a very bright woman in general, one of the things that made her impossible to ignore. Bright makeup, lime-green on her lids, magenta on her lips, and matching finger-nails. She made for an enticing picture, one he found himself struggling to look away from.

"You said to come in and see you before I left?"

"Yes," he said, breaking his focus from her for the first time since she'd come in, looking at the items she'd chucked haphazardly into the chair. He had a very strong urge to straighten them. Hang them on a hook. Anything but simply let them lie there.

"Are you going to fire me?"

"I don't think so," he said, tightening his jaw. "Tell me more about your situation."

A little wrinkle appeared between her brows, her full lips turning down. "In a nutshell, Shyla was my best friend. We moved here together. She got a boyfriend, got pregnant. He left. And everything was fine for a while, because we were working it out together. But she got really sick after giving birth to Ana. She lost a lot of blood during delivery and she had a hard time recovering. She ended up…there was a clot and it traveled to her lungs." She paused and took a breath, her petite shoulders rising and falling with the motion. "She died and that left…Ana and I."

He pushed aside the strange surge of emotion that hit him in the chest. The thought of a motherless child. A mother the child had lost to death. He tightened his jaw. "Your friend's parents?"

"Shyla's mother has never been around. Her father is still alive as far as I know, but he wouldn't be able to care for a child. He wouldn't want to, either."

"And you can't adopt unless you're married."

She let out a long breath and started pacing. "It's not that simple. I mean, she didn't say that absolutely. There's no…

law, or anything. I mean, obviously. But from the moment Rebecca Addler, the caseworker, came to my apartment it was clear that she wasn't thrilled with it."

"What's wrong with your apartment?"

"It's small. I mean, it's nice—it's in a good area, but it's small."

"Housing is expensive in San Diego."

"Yes. Exactly. Expensive. So I have a small apartment, and right now Ana shares a room with me. And I admit that a fifth-floor apartment isn't ideal for raising a child, but plenty of people do it."

"Then why can't you do it?" he asked, frustration starting to grow in his chest, making it feel tight. Making him feel short-tempered.

"I don't know why. But it was really obvious by the way she said…by how she was saying that Ana would be better off with a mother and a father, and didn't I want her to have that? Well, that made it pretty obvious that she really doesn't want me to get custody. And…I panicked."

"And somehow my name came into this? And into the paper?"

Her cheeks turned a deep shade of pink. "I don't know how that happened. The paper. I can't imagine Rebecca… If you could have met her, you would know she didn't do it. Maybe whoever handled the paperwork because I know she made a note."

"A note?"

Paige winced. "Yeah. A note."

"Saying?"

"Your name. That we'd just gotten engaged. She said it was possible it would make a difference."

"You don't think it has more to do with the fact that I'm a billionaire than it has to do with the fact that you're getting married."

He was under no illusion about his charm, or lack of it. And neither was the world in general. The thing that attracted women to him was money. The thing that made him acceptable in the eyes of the social worker would be the same thing. Monetarily, he would be able to provide for a child. Several children, and that *did* matter. A sorry way to decide parentage in his opinion.

But that was the way the world worked. Coming from having none, to having more than he could ever spend, had taught him that in a very effective way.

"Possibly," she said, sucking her bright pink bottom lip into her mouth and worrying it with her teeth.

His phone rang and he punched the speaker button. "Dante Romani."

His assistant's nervous voice filled the room. "Mr. Romani," he said, "the press have been calling all afternoon looking for a statement…about your engagement."

Dante shot Paige his deadliest glare. She didn't shrink. She hardly seemed to notice. She was looking past him, out the window, at the harbor, twirling a lock of hair around her finger, her knees shaking back and forth. She was the most… haphazard creature he'd ever seen.

"What about it?" Dante asked, still unsure how he was going to play it.

As far as the press was concerned, he was marrying Paige and he was adopting a child with her. To go back on that a day later would kill the last vestiges of speculation that he might possess honor or human decency. That wasn't exactly a goal of his. Yes, by the standards of some, he lacked charm. Really, he just wasn't inclined to kiss ass, and he never had been. But it didn't mean he was angling for a complete character assassination by the media, either.

If things got too bad, and they were headed that way, it might affect business. And that was completely unacceptable to him. Don and Mary Colson had adopted an heir to their fortune, to their department store empire, for a reason. It was not so he could let it fail.

And then there was Ana. Dante didn't like children. Didn't

want them. But the memories from his own childhood, memories of foster care, of going from home to home, sometimes good, sometimes not, were strong.

Perhaps Ana would be adopted right away. But would they care for her? Would they love her? Paige did; that much even he could recognize.

This concern, for another human being, was unusual for him. It was foreign. But he couldn't deny that it was there. Very real, very strong. The need to spare an innocent child from some of the potential horrors of life. Horrors he knew far too well.

"They want details," Trevor said.

Dante's eyes locked with Paige's. "Of course they do." *So do I.* "But they'll have to wait. I have no statement at this time." He punched the off button on the phone's intercom. "But I will need one," he said to Paige. A plan was forming in his mind, a way to take this potential PR disaster and turn it into something that would benefit him. But first, he wanted to hear an explanation. "What do you propose we do?"

Paige stopped jiggling her leg. "Get married?" Her expression was so hopeless, so utterly lost looking. "Or…at least let the engagement go on for a while?" The desperation, coming from her in waves, was palpable.

No one had ever cared for him with so much passion, not in the years since he'd lost his birth mother. He didn't regret it. It was far too late in life for that.

But it isn't too late for Ana.

He looked back down at the newspaper. It wouldn't only be for Ana anyway. It was a strange thought…the idea of being able to manipulate the image he'd always had in the press.

He'd grown from sullen teenage boy to feared man all in the eye of the public. For years he'd been painted as an unloving, ungrateful adopted child who had no place in the Colson family. As he'd grown up, his image had changed to that of a hard boss, a heartless lover who drew women in with sexual promises, sensual corruption and money before discarding them. It colored the way people saw him. The way they talked to him. The way they did business with him.

What would it be like to have it change? It wouldn't last, of course. He wouldn't stay with her. Wouldn't pursue anything remotely resembling a real marriage. An engagement though, at least for a while, had interesting possibilities.

But to be seen as the angel rather than the devil…it was an interesting thought. It might make certain transactions easier. Smoother.

Dante was past the point where negative character assessments bothered him. Unless they affected a business. And in the past, he knew people had shied away from dealings with him thanks to his reputation.

A womanizer. Heartless. Cutthroat. Dangerous. It had all been said and then some, most of it spun from speculation and created stories. Would it change things if he were considered settled? A family man? Even if it wasn't permanent, it could quite possibly shift how people saw him.

An interesting thought indeed.

Can she reform him? The real question was, could he use her to reform his image?

For a moment, a brief moment, he allowed himself to think of the many ways he could use her. Fantasies that had been on the edge of his consciousness every time she breezed through the office. Fantasies he had not allowed.

He gave them a moment's time, and then shut the door on them. It was not her body he needed.

"All right, Ms. Harper, for the purposes of keeping the facade, I accept your proposal."

Her blue eyes widened. "You…what?"

"I have decided that I will marry you."

CHAPTER TWO

PAIGE was pretty sure the floor shook underneath her feet. But Dante didn't look at all perturbed, and everything appeared to be stable, so maybe the shaking was all internal.

"You...what?"

"I accept. At least on a surface level. At least until the furor in the media dies down."

"I... Okay," she said, watching her boss as he stood from his position behind his desk. His movements were methodical, planned and purposeful.

He was always like that. Smooth and unruffled. She had wondered, more than once, what it took to get him to loosen up. What it took to shake that perfect, well-ordered control.

She'd wondered, only a couple of times, if a lover ever managed to do it for him. Loosen his tie, run her fingers through his hair.

Now she knew she had the power to do it. Not in the way a lover would, but by inadvertently leaking a fake engagement to the press.

"Excellent," he said, his tone clipped. Decisive. "I see no reason why this can't work."

"I... Why?"

"Is this not what you want? What you need?"

Her head was spinning. This morning everything in her world had been on the verge of collapse, and now—now it seemed like she might actually be able to keep it all standing.

"Well...yes. But let's be honest. You aren't exactly known for your accommodating and helpful nature, sorry, so it seems... out of character."

He bent and picked up the paper from his desk, his dark eyes skimming it. "Can you imagine what the media would say if I backed out? They're already salivating for the chance to rip me to pieces if I would just give it to them. This article is practically a setup for the following piece where they will gleefully report that I have dropped my subordinate fiancée, who I was likely playing power games with, for my own debauched satisfaction, and ruined her chances of adopting her much-loved child. It would have an even darker angle to it, considering I myself am adopted. I can see that headline now."

"Well, yes, I can see how that would be...not good. But I'm surprised they just...believed that we were engaged anyway." *Average woman.* That was what they'd called her in the paper. And Dante Romani would never be linked with a woman who was average.

In so many ways it was like a bad joke. A cruel high school flashback.

"Been reading stories about me?" he asked, his lips curving into a half smile.

"Well, I mean, I see them," she said, stuttering. He didn't need to know that sometimes she looked at pictures of him for a little longer than necessary. It wasn't like anyone could blame her. She was a woman; he was a stunningly attractive man. But she knew she had no shot with him, ever. And no desire to take one. "But also, we haven't really been seen together in public, so it seems odd that they would just assume, based on a random tip, that we're engaged."

He shrugged. "It sounds like something I would do. Keep a real relationship under wraps. In theory. I haven't had one, so I wouldn't know."

"Right. Yes. I know that."

"You do read the stories, then."

Her cheeks heated and she cleared her throat. "That and I have keen powers of observation and… Oh, no!"

"What?"

Paige looked at the clock on Dante's wall, positioned just above his head. "I have to go pick Ana up. Everyone is probably waiting on me."

"I'll come with you," he said.

"What?" She needed to get away from him for a minute. Or have flustered-angry Dante back. Now that he had a plan he had taken firm control over everything and it was making her feel dazed.

"Well, I am your fiancé now, am I not?"

Paige's head was swimming, her fingers feeling slightly numb. "I don't know…are you?"

He nodded once. "Yes. For all intents and purposes."

"Oookay then."

"You seem uncertain, Paige," he said, taking his coat off the peg that was mounted to the wall and opening the door.

Paige scrambled to collect her things from the chair. "I…I'm not, not really. I just don't know how you went from spitting nails in my office to…agreeing."

"I'm a man of action. I don't have time to be indecisive."

She walked past him and out into the lobby area of his floor. His assistant, Trevor, was positioned behind his desk, his eyes locked on to the both of them.

"Have a nice evening, Mr. Romani," he said.

"You too, Trevor. You should go home," Dante said.

"In a bit. So…"

"Oh, yeah," Paige said. "We're engaged."

"You are?" he asked, his expression skeptical.

Paige nodded and looked at Dante who looked…uncharacteristically amused. "Yes," she said.

He nodded. "Yes."

"I…didn't know," Trevor said.

"I'm a private man," Dante said. "When it suits me."

"Apparently," Trevor said, looking back at his computer screen.

"See you tomorrow," Dante said. Trevor made a vague nod in acknowledgment.

Paige followed Dante to the elevator and stepped inside when the doors opened. "So…Trevor doesn't seem thrilled," she said. Really, she was surprised at the dynamic between Dante and his assistant. Dante was something of a fearsome figure in her mind, and the fact that Trevor hadn't been fired on the spot for his obvious annoyance with the situation wasn't exactly what she'd expected.

"Trevor is mad because he didn't know," Dante said. "Because he likes to know everything, and make sure it's jotted down in my schedule at least six months in advance."

"And you don't mind that he was…upset?"

Dante frowned. "Why? Did you expect me to throw him from the thirtieth-floor window?"

"It was a possibility I hadn't ruled out."

"I'm not a tyrant."

"No?" He gave her a hard stare. "Well, you fired Carl Johnson. For the baseball game," she said.

"And it makes me a tyrant because I expect my employees to show up during work hours and earn the generous salaries I pay them?" he asked.

"Well…it was for his child's T-ball game…"

"That meant nothing to anyone else in the meeting. It might have personally meant something to Carl, but not to anyone else. And if everyone was allowed to miss work anytime something seemed like it might take precedence for them personally, we would not be able to get anything done."

"Well, what about when you have something in your personal life that requires attention."

"I have neatly handled what might have been a dilemma by having no personal life," he said, his tone hard.

"Oh. Well…"

"You expect me to be unreasonable because of what is

written about me," he said, "in spite of what you see in the office on a daily basis. Which only serves to prove the power of the media. And the fact that it's time I manipulated it to my advantage."

Her face burned. "I…suppose." It was true. Dante was a hard man but, other than this morning, she'd never heard him raise his voice. As bosses went, he'd never been a bad one. But she'd always gotten an illicit thrill when he was around. A sense of something dark. And it was very likely the media was to blame.

"And you *do* read the stories they write about me," he said, as if he was able to read her mind.

She pursed her lips. "Fine. I've read some of what's been written about you."

"Being a tyrant implies a lack of control, in my opinion, Paige. And it shows an attempt to claim it in a very base way. I have control over this company, of my business, in all situations, and I don't have to raise my voice to get it."

She cleared her throat and stared straight ahead at the closed elevator door. At their warped reflections in the gleaming metal. She came just past his shoulder, and that was in her killer heels. She looked…tiny. A bit awkward. And he looked…well, like Dante always looked. Dark and delicious, supremely masculine, completely not awkward and just a little frightening.

"You raised your voice when you were in my office," she said, still looking at reflection Dante, and not actual Dante. Actual Dante was almost too handsome to look at directly, especially when standing so close to him.

He laughed, a short, one-note sound. "It was deserved in the situation, don't you think?"

"Was it?"

"How would you have felt if the situations were reversed?"

"I don't know. Look, are you serious about this?" she asked, turning to face him just as the doors to their floor slid open.

"I don't joke very often, if at all," he said.

"Well, that's true. But in my experience when men say they want to date me, it can turn out to have been a cruel joke, so I'm thinking my boss agreeing to get engaged to me could be something along those same lines."

"What is this?"

She shook her head. "Nothing, just…high school. You are planning on following through with this, right? Dante, if I get caught—committing fraud, basically—it might not just be Ana that I lose."

"As previously stated, Paige, I do not joke. I am not joking now."

"I just don't understand why you're helping me."

"Because it helps me."

He said it with such certainty, and no shame.

Paige sputtered. "In what regard?"

"People see me…well, as a tyrant. If not that, a corruptor of innocents, and perhaps, the personification of Charon, ready to lead people down the river Styx and into Hades."

He said it lightly, with some amusement, though his expression stayed smooth. Paige laughed. "Uh, yes, well, I suppose that's true."

"Already there is speculation that you might manage to reform me. The idea of giving that impression…I find it intriguing. An interesting social experiment if nothing else, and one with the potential to improve business for me."

"Of course you would also actually be helping me and Ana," she pointed out.

He nodded once. "I don't find that objectionable."

She could have laughed. He said it so seriously, as if she might really think he would find helping others something vile. And he said it like that perception didn't bother him.

"Okay. Good." She continued on down the hall with him, on the way to the day care center that she'd come to be so grateful for.

She opened the door and sighed heavily when she saw

Genevieve, the main caregiver, holding Ana. They were the last two there. "I'm so sorry," she said, dumping her things on the counter and reaching for Ana.

Genevieve smiled. "No worries. She's almost asleep again. She did scream a little bit when five rolled around and you weren't here."

Paige frowned, a sharp pain hitting her in the chest. Ana was only four months old, but she already knew Paige as her mother. There had been such few moments in Paige's life when she'd been certain of something, where she hadn't felt restless and on the verge of failure.

One of those moments was when she'd been hired to design the window displays for Colson's. The other was when Shyla had placed Ana in Paige's arms.

Can you take care of her?

She'd only meant for a moment. While she rested and tried to shake some of the chronic fatigue that came with having a newborn. But Shyla had lain down on their sofa for a nap that day and never woken up. And Paige was still taking care of Ana. Because she had to. Because she wanted to. Because she loved Ana more than her own life.

Genevieve transferred Ana and her blanket into Paige's arms, and Paige pulled her daughter in close, her heart melting, her eyes stinging. She looked back at Dante, and she knew that she'd done the right thing.

Because she would be damned if anyone was taking Ana from her, and she would do whatever she had to do to insure that no one did. Ana was hers forever. And even if marriage to Dante wasn't strictly necessary, she would take it as insurance every time.

Genevieve bent to retrieve Ana's diaper bag, then popped back up, her eyes widening when she registered the presence of their boss. "Mr. Romani, what brings you down here?"

Paige thought the girl had a slightly hopeful edge to her voice. As if she was hoping Dante had come to ravish her against the wall. Something Paige could kind of relate to, since Dante had that effect. Even Paige, who knew better than to fantasize about men who were so far out of her league, struggled with the odd Dante-themed fantasy. It was involuntary, really.

"I'm here to collect Ana," he said.

Genevieve looked confused. "Oh...I..." He reached over the counter and took the diaper bag from the surprised-looking Genevieve.

"With Paige," he finished. "It was announced in the news today, but in case you haven't heard, Paige and I are to be married."

Genevieve's mouth dropped open. "Oh, I..."

"Let's go, *cara mia*," he said, sweeping Paige's things from the counter and gathering them into his arms. Her big, broad-chested Italian boss, clutching her sequined purse to his chest, was enough to make her dissolve into hysteric fits of laughter, but there was something else, another feeling, one that made her stomach tight and her chest warm, stopping the giggles.

She wiggled her fingers in Genevieve's direction and walked through the door, which Dante was currently holding open for her with his shoulder.

Paige continued down the hall, heading toward the parking garage. Dante was behind her, still holding all of her things. She stopped. "Sorry, I can take that."

"I've got it," he said.

"But you don't have to...I mean...you don't have to walk me out to my car."

"I think I do," he said.

"No. You really don't. There's no reason."

"We have just announced our engagement. Do you think I would let my fiancée walk out to her car by herself, with a baby, a diaper bag, a purse and...whatever else I'm currently holding?"

"Maybe not," she said. "But then, you don't really have a reputation for being chivalrous."

"Perhaps not," he said, "but I'm changing it, remember?"

"Why exactly?"

"Walk while you talk," he said.

Not for the first time, Paige noticed that he didn't look at Ana. She seemed no more interesting to him than the inanimate objects in his arms. Most people softened when they saw her, reached out and touched her cheek or hair. Not Dante.

"Okay," she said, turning away from him and continuing on. "So…how are we going to do this?" she asked.

She paused at the door, a strange, new habit she seemed to have developed just since coming down from the top floor with Dante. And he didn't let her down. He reached past her and opened the door, holding it for her as she walked into the parking garage.

"Where are you parked?" he asked.

"There," she said, flicking her head to the right. "I get to park close now because of Ana."

"Nice policy," he said. "I don't believe I was responsible for it."

"I think your father was."

A strange expression passed over his face. "Interesting. But very like Don. He's always been very practical. One reason he put in the day care facility early on. Because he knew that employees with children needed to feel like their family concerns were a priority. And better for the company because it ensures that there will be minimal issues with employees missing work because of child care concerns. Of course, missing baseball games cannot be helped sometimes, and I am not putting a field in the parking garage," he finished dryly.

"I imagine not." She shifted, not quite sure what to do next. "Well, I've never met your father, but judging by some of the policies here, he's a very good man."

Dante nodded. "He is."

Paige turned and headed toward her car. "Oh…purse," she said, stopping her progress and turning to look at Dante. He started trying to extricate the glittery bag from the pile in his arms. Then she checked the door. "Never mind, I forgot to lock it."

"You forgot to lock it?"

"It's secure down here," she said, pulling the back door open and depositing the sleeping Ana in her seat.

"Locking it would make it doubly secure," he said, his tone stiff.

She straightened. "How long have you lived in this country?"

He frowned. "Since I was six. Why?"

"You just…you speak very formal English."

"It's my second language. And anyway, Don and Mary speak very formal English. They are quite upper-crust, you know."

"And you call them by their first names?"

"I was fourteen when they adopted me, which I'm sure you know given your proclivity for tabloids."

"Wow. Exaggerate much? Proclivity…"

"And," he continued as if she hadn't spoken, "it would have seemed strange to call them anything other than their first names. I was adopted to be the heir to the Colson empire, more than I was adopted to be a son."

"Is that what they told you?"

His expression didn't alter. "It's the only reason I can think of."

"Then why aren't you a Colson?" She'd often wondered that, but she'd never asked, of course. Partly because until today she'd never had more than a moment to speak to him.

"Something Don and I agreed on from the start. I wished to keep my mother's name."

"Not your father's?"

His face hardened, his dark eyes black, blank. "No."

Paige blinked. "Oh." She looked back down at Ana, who was sleeping soundly and was buckled tightly into her seat. She closed the door and leaned against the side of the car. "So…I guess I'll see you tomorrow then."

"You'll see me tonight," he said, turning away from her.

"What?"

"We're not going into this without a plan. And if I'm going to help you, you will help me. It's in both of our best interests that it look real, once we take one step into confirming this, there is no going back. You understand?"

She nodded slowly.

"And you need to remember this. It's essential for you, much more than it is for me. If this blows up it would simply be another bruise on my reputation, and frankly, what's one more beating in that area? You on the other hand…"

"I could lose everything," she said, a sharp pang of regret hitting her in the stomach.

"So we'll make sure we don't misstep," he said. "I'll follow you to your apartment."

The thought of him, so big and masculine and…orderly, in her tiny, cluttered space, made her feel edgy. Of having a man, any man really, but a man like him specifically, in her space, was so foreign. But really, there was no other option. And she couldn't act like he made her nervous. He was supposed to be her fiancé.

And people were somehow supposed to believe that he had chosen her.

"I feel dizzy," she said.

He frowned. "Should I drive?"

She shook her head. "I'll be fine," she said, opening the driver's side door. "I'll be fine," she repeated again, for her own benefit more than his.

And she really hoped it was true.

CHAPTER THREE

PAIGE'S house was very like her. Bright, disordered and a bit manic. The living area was packed with things. Canvases, mannequins, bolts of fabric. There was a large bookshelf at the back wall filled with bins. Bins of beads, sequins and other things that sparkled. Her office had simply been the tip of the iceberg.

This was the glittery underbelly.

"Sorry about the mess," she said. "You can just dump my stuff on the couch." She set the baby's car seat gently on the coffee table and bent, unbuckling the little girl from her seat, drawing her to her chest.

He looked away from the scene. Watching her with the baby reminded him of things. He wasn't even sure what things exactly, because every time a piece of memory tried to push into his mind, he pushed it out.

He focused instead on trying to find a hook of some kind, something to hang her bag on at least.

"Just dump it," she said, shifting Ana in her arms.

"I don't…dump things," he said tightly.

She rolled her eyes. "Then hold Ana while I do it."

He drew back, discomfort tightening his throat. "I don't hold babies."

She rolled her eyes. "Pick one," she said.

He set her purse on her kitchen counter and then went farther into the living room, depositing her fabric on another pile of fabric, and placing her sketchbook next to a bin that had paints and pencils in it.

That had some reason to it, at least.

She laughed. "You couldn't do it. You couldn't just dump it."

"There's nothing wrong with caring for what you have."

"I do care for it."

"How do you find everything in here?"

She cocked her head to the side and he caught sight of the flash of pink buried in her hair again. "Easily." She put her hand on Ana's back and patted her absently, pacing across the living room.

There was no denying that she looked at ease in her surroundings, even if he couldn't fathom it. He needed order. A space for everything. A clear and obvious space for himself. He prized it, above almost everything else.

He cleared his throat. "What size ring do you wear?"

"Six," she said, frowning. "Why?"

"You need one."

"Well, I have rings. I can just wear one of those," she said, waving her hand in dismissal.

"You do not have the sort of ring I would buy the woman I intended to marry."

She paused her pacing. "Well, maybe you wouldn't buy the sort of ring I would want."

"We'll come to a compromise, but your engagement ring must be up to my standards."

She groaned and sank onto the couch, baby Ana still resting against her chest. "This is bizarre."

"You're the one who said we were engaged."

"Yes. I know. And I knew the minute I said it I was in over my head but it just...popped out."

For some reason, he didn't doubt her. Probably because he was the least logical option to choose. If she'd been thinking, she would have chosen a different man. One who liked children and puppies and had some semblance of compassion.

He was not that man, and he knew it as well as everyone around him.

"I can't lose her," she said, her focus on the baby in her arms. "I can't let one stupid mistake ruin her life. And mine."

He looked at Paige, at the baby nestled against her, ignoring the piece of his brain that demanded he look away from the scene of maternal love. Ana took a deep breath, almost a sigh, that lifted her tiny shoulders and shook her whole little frame. She was content, at rest, against the woman she knew as her mother.

Unexpectedly, genuine concern wrenched his gut. It was foreign. Emotion, in general, was foreign to him. But this kind even more so.

"I understand," he said. And he found that he did. "But that means this can't just look real, it has to be real."

It occurred to him, just as he spoke the words. The engagement wouldn't be enough. It would have to be more. It would have to be marriage.

"You want to keep Ana."

"More than anything," she said.

"Then we have to be sure that the adoption is final before we go our separate ways. We need to get married, not just get engaged."

She blinked twice. "Like…really get married?"

"I think a government office would be especially concerned with the legality of our union so we can't very well jump over a broom on the beach."

"But…but a real marriage?"

"Of course."

Her blue eyes widened. "What do you mean by that?"

He almost laughed at the abject horror evident in her expression. Most women didn't look horrified if it was implied they might sleep together; on the contrary, he was used to women being eager to accept the invitation or eager to seek him out.

Though he turned his share down. Far too many were out

to reform the bad boy. To make the man with the heart of stone care, to reach him, save him, perhaps. Something that simply wasn't possible.

He wasn't a sadist and he had no interest in hurting people. He could easily take advantage of wide-eyed innocents with a desire to reform him. But he didn't. He wouldn't.

Still, he found Paige's clear aversion to it interesting.

"I don't mean in that way," he said.

Her blue eyes widened further. "What way?" As if she had to prove her thoughts hadn't even gotten near the bedroom door. She was a very cute, unconvincing liar.

"I don't intend to sleep with you." Even as he said it, he wondered if the underwear she had on beneath her clothes was a bright as the rest of her. Bright pink, showing hints of pale skin beneath delicate lace? He could imagine laying her down on white sheets, the filmy garments electric against the pristine backdrop.

Color flooded her cheeks and she looked down at the top of Ana's head. "I…of course not. I mean…I never thought you did."

He shouldn't. He shouldn't be toying with fantasies of it, either. He had to stay focused. He tightened down on the vein that seemed to bleed a never-ending flow of erotic, Paige-themed imagery through his brain.

"The look on your face said otherwise."

"It was just an honest question. And anyway, you're taking this a step deeper, and I'm entitled to ask some questions, and I just need to know what 'real' would mean to you. Other than the license, I guess."

"What I mean by it being real, has to do with our activities outside the bedroom. You will need to accompany me to any events I might need to attend. We will have to get married, and you will have to move into my home. It has to look real."

Dante didn't like the idea of it. Not in the least. Of bringing this little rainbow whirlwind into his personal space. And not just Paige, but the baby, as well.

He gritted his teeth. His house was big. It would be fine. And it would be temporary. He didn't question the decisions he made. He simply made them.

She nodded slowly. "I know. But I mean…it seems crazy and extreme."

"It's hardly extreme. Understand this, Paige, you've gotten us both into a bit of a dangerous game. There could be very real consequences if we're caught in the lie. Very real for you, especially."

She looked away, pulling her lush bottom lip between her teeth. "You're right."

He pulled his focus away from her mouth. "Of course I am. Do you have anything to drink?"

"Uh…there's a box of wine in the fridge."

Dante didn't bother to keep the disapproval from showing on his face. "A box?"

"Yeah," she said. "Sorry if that doesn't meet with your standards. Maybe you can choose me some wine and a ring?"

"I'm not opposed to it. However, when you move into my home, there will be a wine selection waiting for you. And none of it will be boxed."

"Well, la-dee-da," she said, standing. "I'm going to put Ana in her crib. Do you think you can stand here for a minute and keep the internal judgment to a minimum?"

"I'll do my best," he said drily.

He watched her walk out of the room, his eyes drawn to the sway of her hips and the rounded curve of her butt. He was only human, and she was beautiful. Not his type in the least, and yet, it wasn't the first time he'd noticed her.

He liked women who were cool. Contained. In both looks and manner. And Paige was none of those things, which made her both a fascination and impossible to ignore.

Paige returned a moment later, hands free, a wet spot on her shirt near her shoulder. "You have something on your shirt," he said.

She looked down. "Oh. Yeah. She's really drooly right now. No teeth to hold it back."

He let out a long breath and sat down on the couch. "I think I will take some wine."

The idea of having this woman and her explosion of belongings and a baby who was, by Paige's description, drooly, in his home was enough to send a kick of anxiety through him.

Paige shrugged and headed to the kitchen, reaching up into a high cabinet and taking down two mismatched pieces of stemware. A green champagne flute and a clear wine goblet. Then she opened up the fridge and bent down, dispensing wine from the plastic tap that was jammed into the cardboard box, into the cups.

She kicked her shoes off and pushed them to the side as she walked to the couch, wineglasses in her hands. "I haven't had anyone over in a long time. You know, other than the social worker." She handed him the clear glass and moved to a chair that was positioned next to the couch. She sat down on her knees, her feet tucked up under her.

"In how long?"

Paige looked down into her wine. "Since Shyla died."

"That must have been difficult." It was hard for him to find the words you were supposed to say when people were grieving. Hard to know what they wanted to hear. He had experience dealing with death, and yet, he couldn't remember what people had said to him. If they had said anything.

Paige took a sip of her wine and nodded. "Yes. She was my best friend. She and I moved to San Diego from Oregon together shortly after we graduated."

"Why here?"

She shrugged. "It's sunny? I don't know. A chance to start over, I guess. Be new people. She met her boyfriend really soon after we got here, and she ended up moving in with him. Then she got pregnant and he freaked out. And I had her move in with me. It was crowded but great. And then…

and then Ana was born and it was so fun to have her here. So amazing." Paige looked down into her glass, tears sparkling on her lashes like shattered crystal. "We were making it work. The three of us."

"How old are you, Paige?" he asked. She looked young. Beneath all the makeup, he was sure she looked like a girl who could still be in school. Her skin was smooth and pale, her blue eyes round, fringed with long, dark lashes. Her lips were full and pink, turned down at the corners, giving the illusion of a slight pout.

"Twenty-two."

"You're only twenty-two?" Ten years younger than he was. And yet she was willing to take on raising a child by herself. "Then why do you want to raise a child right now? You have so many years ahead of you. And don't you want to get married?"

She shrugged. "Not really. And anyway, I guess…no this isn't the ideal time for me to have a baby. And if you had asked me a few months ago if I was ready to have a baby, I would have told you no. But that would be a hypothetical baby. And Ana isn't hypothetical. She's here. And she doesn't have anyone. Her birth mother is dead, my friend, my best friend is dead. The line on the birth certificate that should have a father's name on it is blank. She needs me."

"She needs anyone who will care for her. It doesn't have to be you." She flinched when he said the words.

"It does," she said, her voice thin.

"Why?"

"I don't know for sure if anyone else will love her like I do. And I…I knew Shyla. I knew her better than anyone, and she knew me. I'll be able to tell her about her mother." Paige's throat convulsed. "And Shyla asked me to. She asked me to take care of her."

That answer hit him hard in the chest and the memories he'd been pushing away from the moment they'd picked Ana up at the nursery crowded in, too fast and forceful for him to hold back anymore. He'd been much older than Ana when he'd lost his mother, so he remembered a lot on his own. Memories that he often wished he didn't have. Of soft lullabies, gentle hands...and blood. In the end...so much blood.

He blinked and shook off the memory, reclaiming control, lifting the glass of wine to his lips and grimacing when the chilled, acrid liquid hit his tongue. There was no buzz on earth worth that. He set it back down on the table.

"I understand that."

"It's not just for her. It's for me, too. I love her. Like... like she really is my baby. I saw her come into the world. I cared for her from the start, did the midnight feedings and visits to the doctor. I can't...I can't just let her go. Let her go to someone else. Someone who might not love her like I do. How could anyone love her like I do? I love her so much that sometimes it overwhelms me."

Paige spoke with conviction, so much it vibrated from her petite frame. Dante couldn't imagine emotion like that. It was so far beyond where he was now.

In truth, he couldn't imagine a good emotion that strong. Fear, grief, the type that had the power to reduce a man to a quivering, raw mass of anguish...that he knew. But nothing like it since. Nothing that even came close. He was numb to feeling.

But he could sense hers, could feel them radiating off her. She didn't hide them, didn't sublimate them to try to deal with them. He doubted she could. She was too honest.

Well, except for that one little lie. The one he was currently enmeshed in.

"You cannot keep the pink in your hair," he said. He needed to tone her down, to make her less distracting.

"What?" she sifted her fingers through her dark hair, the movement unconsciously sexy.

"I would hardly become engaged to a woman with pink hair."

"Um...but you did. You totally just did."

"I didn't know about the pink stripe until recently. When I found out I nearly broke it off with you, so you promised to go to the hairdresser."

"You can't even see it if I have my hair down."

"I saw it when we were in bed." Again, the images of her skin against his sheets hit him hard.

Her cheeks colored a deep rose. He couldn't remember the last time he'd made a woman blush, discounting Paige, and he certainly couldn't remember ever finding it so fascinating.

"Uh…and that was your predominant thought? My pink hair? We did something wrong, in that case." She looked away from him and took another long drink of her vile wine.

"Just color over it," he said.

"I have an appointment in a few weeks. It'll keep."

"You seem to forget that I'm doing you a favor."

"I didn't think that was your predominant motivation. And anyway, I'm doing you a favor, too."

He shrugged. "Maybe. Maybe not. I don't know what the reaction will be. I'm curious to find out."

"So, this is just a social experiment to you?"

"It's interesting, yes. Ultimately though, it's with a mind to improving business."

"And deceiving people doesn't bother you?"

"Does it bother you?"

She frowned. "Usually. But not now. Not for…not for Ana. I would do anything for her."

"So I gathered."

"I'm far more bothered by the fact that we're actually… that we'll be getting married." She looked down, giving him a view of long, dark lashes spread over pale skin, and lids that were lined in emerald green, a sprinkling of golden glitter adding sparkle.

"If you can think of another way…"

She raised her focus, her expression open, honest. "I can't. Nothing this certain."

"Then don't trouble yourself over it."

She frowned. "I won't. So, now what do we do?"

"I'll text your ring size to Trevor and send him to procure something suitable. You will have it on your desk by lunch. Then…then we have a charity event to go to."

"I don't have anyone to watch Ana."

"I'll pay Genevieve to do it. She's good with Ana, isn't she?"

"Well, yes, but…I'll have been away from her all day."

"Leave early," he said. "I'll come here and pick you up before the event."

"Why do you keep having answers to all of my problems?" she asked, her tone petulant.

"I would think that would be a good thing, especially since you have so many problems at the moment."

She let out an exasperated sigh. "Granted."

He stood, taking his glass of nearly untouched wine off the coffee table. "Good night, then. I'll be by to pick you and Ana up at seven-thirty tomorrow morning."

"Wait…pick me up?"

"You're my woman now, Paige, and that comes with a certain set of expectations."

She blinked. "I didn't…I didn't agree to this."

"You brought me into this. That means you aren't making all the rules anymore." He turned and walked into the kitchen, pausing at the sink and dumping the contents of his glass down the drain. "That wine is unforgivable. I will teach you to like good wine."

"And you'll teach me to like good jewelry, and the sort of hair you deem 'good.' Tell me, Dante, what else will you teach me to like?" She crossed her arms beneath her breasts—rather generous breasts—and a rush of heat assailed him. Intense. Impossible to ignore.

The desire to lean in and trace her lips with his fingertip, with his tongue, was nearly too strong for him to overcome. But he would. He would keep control, as he always did.

He took one last, lingering look, at her pink lips. "That's a very dangerous question, Paige," he said. "Very dangerous."

CHAPTER FOUR

THAT'S a very dangerous question.

Yes, it had been a dangerous question. Only Paige hadn't realized just how dangerous until it had come out of her mouth. And she was certain that Dante didn't realize how much truth was behind it. How much teaching she would need.

Oh, dear.

Just thinking about it again made her feel hot, all over. And that was exactly why she wasn't going to think about her futile, one-sided attraction anymore

She looked at the clock and shifted in her chair. Genevieve was already here, and Ana had been happily passed off to her. It hadn't taken the little girl more than a moment to recognize her daily caregiver and the two were happily playing on the rug in the living room.

Paige sighed and realized that she was jiggling her leg. She stopped herself. Her little nervous habit wasn't a good look with the long, silky gown she was wearing.

Yes, she was wearing a dress, to go on a date. Which was something she hadn't done in…almost ever. She wasn't the girl that men went after. She was the screwup, the funny one. The one with a pink stripe in her hair, although Dante was putting the kibosh on that.

She didn't get dressed up in slinky gowns to go to fancy charity dinners with billionaires. She also didn't get engaged to billionaires. Oh, yeah, she didn't really marry them, either, though that was now in her future. All because her stupid, impulsive brain had spit out the most ridiculous lie at the worst time.

Desperation wasn't her best state. She more or less had a handle on the blurting these days. When she'd been a kid, all the way up into high school, it had been really bad. She was always saying stupid things and embarrassing herself, which was one reason she'd opted for class clown rather than trying to be sexy or cool or anything like that. Letting it go, instead of wishing she could be something she wasn't, had been much easier.

Or rather, as the case had been, she'd had one incredibly defining, humiliating moment that never let her forget that there were certain guys, who liked certain kinds of girls. And she was not one of them.

There was a heavy knock at her door and she scrambled up out of the chair, grabbing her handbag and wrap. She scurried into the living room and bent down, dropping a kiss onto Ana's soft, fuzzy head.

"I won't be too late," she said to Genevieve.

"I wouldn't blame you if you were," Genevieve said.

Paige's cheeks got hot and she was sure they were a lovely shade of red. "I…we won't be late." She had to get a handle on the blushing, too. There was no reason to blush. Dante Romani was hardly going to ravish her in the back of his car.

She straightened and draped her bright purple wrap over her bare shoulders, giving herself a little look in the small mirror that hung in her living room on her way to the door of her apartment.

The door opened just as she reached it.

"Were you going to leave me freezing on the front step?"

"It's San Diego. It's not freezing. And you're in the temperature-controlled hallway."

"It's the principle," he said.

"I had to say goodbye to Ana. Do you want to see her?"

A strange look crossed his face. Confusion, fear, then boredom. "No."

"Oh, sorry. Most people like babies, you know," she said, stepping out into the hall, closing the door behind her.

"I have no interest in having any of my own. I'm not certain why it would be important for me to like babies."

"They're cute."

"Yes, so are puppies but I don't want one."

"A baby isn't a puppy," she said.

He shrugged. "It doesn't matter to me for the reason previously stated."

She rolled her eyes and pushed the button on the elevator. "Right. Well. I hope Ana and I don't disturb you too much when we live in your home, as you don't want a wife or a child."

"It's a large house," he said, his words carrying a stiff undertone, as if he didn't believe it would be large enough.

The doors to the elevator slid open and they both stepped inside. She'd never noticed how small elevators really were before she'd taken to riding in them with Dante Romani. He made everything feel smaller. Tighter. Because he filled the space he was in so absolutely.

It wasn't just because he was well over six feet tall and broad, either. It was his charisma, the dark energy that radiated from him. He was so unobtainable, so uninterested in what was happening around him. It made you want to go and grab his attention. Made you want to be in his sphere. To make him seem interested. To make him smile.

To make him laugh.

At least she did, but she was good at that. Making people laugh and smile. Defusing tension with antics and jokes. And she had, apparently, not learned her lesson about unobtainable men.

She nearly opened her mouth to make one when her eyes locked with his and the breath leached from her body.

His dark eyes roamed over her curves, taking in every

inch of her. And she was reminded again of their exchange last night.

What else will you teach me to like?

Oh, no, no, no. She wasn't going there. She never had before, no reason to start now.

Besides, Dante could have any woman he wanted, on the terms he chose. He had no reason to start lusting after her pink-striped self.

She'd grown up in a small town, and every guy she knew had known her from the time they were in kindergarten together. They knew that she talked too much, and that she very often laughed too loud. That she had trouble paying attention in class. That she'd cut a boy's tongue with her braces during her first kiss. They knew that she'd been the focus of what had essentially been the senior prank. They knew that she'd barely passed high school, that her parents hadn't seen the point of paying for her to go to college when she just wouldn't apply herself. They'd watched her get a job at a coffee shop instead of going away to school like everyone else.

They had all watched her grow from an awkward kid, to an awkward teen, to an awkward adult. It was like living in a fishbowl. And being the slow fish with the crippled fin. Nothing like her straight-A achieving sister and her football-star brother.

She was just…Paige. And it had always seemed like a pitifully small accomplishment, just being her. For most of her life, she'd accepted it. She'd just put on the image they'd applied to her and owned it. So much easier than trying to be anything else.

But there was a point, as she was pouring a cup of coffee for her fiftieth customer of the day, who asked her about her brother or sister, and not about her, that she couldn't do it anymore.

A week later she'd moved. Just so she could be new to a place. So she had a hope of finding who she was apart from the painful averageness that marked her life.

It hadn't been an instant transformation, no sudden rise to the top of the social heap. But she'd made a small group of friends. She'd found her job at Colson's. That provided her with the first real sense of pride she'd ever had in a job.

They'd seen her raw talent and they'd hired her based on that, not based on classroom performance. Colson's, and by extension, Dante, was her first experience with being believed in.

Strange.

She cast him a sideways glance. He was tall and...rigid in his tux. Each line of his suit jacket conforming to his physique with precision. Dante was never ruffled. She envied that a little bit. Or a lot of a bit, truth be told. She was captivated by it, really, his control. His perfection. His beauty. It was a dark, masculine beauty, nothing soft or traditionally pretty about him. It made her want to look at him, and keep looking.

The elevator doors slid open and they walked out of her apartment building and to the street. There was a black car parked against the curb, waiting for them, she assumed.

Dante opened the back door for her and she slid inside. She'd never ridden in a car with a driver before. Not even a taxi. She always drove her own seen-better-days car.

"It will be nice not being the one fighting traffic for a change," she said when Dante got in on the other side and settled into the seat beside her.

"Mmm," he said, taking his phone out of his pocket and devoting his attention to checking his email.

And just like that, the hot guy wasn't looking at her anymore. Typical.

She let her gaze wander to her left hand, to her still-bare ring finger. "Oh...didn't you...you were going to give me a ring before tonight, weren't you?"

He set his phone down. "Yes," he said. "I don't know why you're intent on spoiling the surprise."

"Uh...because it's not a surprise."

"Perhaps I had something planned."

She didn't think he was serious. But with Dante it was hard to tell. Still, she couldn't help but wonder what it would be like, to have a man like him do the get-down-on-one-knee thing and ask her to be his wife. To look at her with intensity in those dark eyes and...

"So, ring?" She held out her hand and tried to shut out the little fantasy that was playing in the back of her mind.

Forget a dream proposal. She should aim for a kiss that wasn't a disaster first.

Her reached into the inner pocket of his suit jacket and produced a velvet box. "Be my wife, et cetera," he said, opening the box, revealing a pear-shaped emerald surrounded by diamonds.

"It's...wow." Hard not to be completely floored when a gorgeous man was giving you a beautiful ring. "How did you know I liked green?"

"Your eye shadow," he said.

She looked up, as if she could see it. "Oh."

"And I thought the color and style would suit you. Sedate doesn't seem to be your thing."

"Uh...no. Not so much."

"Put it on," he said.

"What? Oh, yeah." She looked down at the ring and a clawing sense of dread made her chest tighten. Was she really going to do this? To put on his ring and go all the way with this?

Yes. Yes, she was. She'd never believed in anything more in her whole life. She'd never been the goal-oriented one in her family. She'd never been the top achiever. She'd never wanted anything so much it made her ache.

That wasn't the case now. Now there was Ana. And she made Paige want to be the best mother. Made her want to do everything she could to give her baby the best life possible. To encourage her, to love her as she was.

She took a deep breath and lifted the ring from its silken

nest, sliding it onto her finger. "There. We're engaged now," she said.

He nodded slowly and leaned back in the seat. She couldn't tell what he was thinking. If he was thinking.

"What?" she asked.

"What do you mean by that?"

"I was just wondering what you were thinking. I mean… this is weird." She wondered if he was thinking of a beautiful blonde, or stunning, dark-haired beauty he would rather have given a ring to. The thought made her chest feel odd. Tight. "We don't really know each other and…were you planning on getting married ever?"

"No," he said, definitively. Decisively.

"Oh. Not even if you meet the right person?"

"There is no right person for me. Or at least not one who's right for more than a couple of days. And nights."

Dante watched Paige's face, the confusion, the little bit of judgment. What he'd just said wasn't true in the strictest sense. The part about marriage was true, but the way he'd spoken of his relationships made it sound like he and the women he slept with met and spent a few days locked in a passionate embrace.

Nothing could be further from the truth.

He'd had arrangements with a few different women over the course of his adult life. Women who were just as busy and driven as he was. Women who were just as averse to relationships.

The women he usually took to the charity events, the models, the actresses…he didn't sleep with them. They were the bit of flash, the ones who looked good in pictures and who wanted to be in them.

But they were too young, many of then. Too starry-eyed and not nearly cynical enough. The women he took to bed, all they wanted was a couple of hours and a couple of orgasms. They wanted what he wanted. They didn't want forever and fireworks; they wanted a basic need to be met. And that's what happened. Basic, simple pursuit of release.

Still, there was no way to explain that without making it sound even worse.

And when had he ever cared what anyone thought? Never. He'd come into the public eye amid speculation and criticism. The Italian orphan that had somehow weaseled his way into the Colson family. That had been named as the heir of a billion-dollar fortune. There had been endless speculation about him, about how it had happened. As if he, even at fourteen, had known some sort of dark secret about the older couple who had taken him into their home. Something that would have enticed them to take on such a sullen, angry child.

He had never once tried to correct the rumors.

But something about the look in Paige's eyes made him want to clarify, to change her assumptions. Or at least make an excuse.

"What about you," he asked, happy to redirect the focus of the conversation to her. "Do you want to get married? Beyond this, I mean."

"Well, I wasn't really at the point where I was thinking about it."

"All women think about it."

"That's a gross generalization and there's no way you can know that. Or rather, you *can* know that you're wrong because I wasn't. Not in a serious way."

"Why not?"

"I've been too busy discovering who I am. Apart from the small town I grew up in, I mean. I've been down here for about three years and I've been kind of…finding myself. Which sounds maybe a little bit geeky but it's true. Back at home there were all these preconceived ideas about me. Who I was, what I was capable of. And when the town is as small as mine, those ideas don't just come from your parents, they come from…everyone. I moved here and decided to really figure out who I would be if there was no one around expect-ing anything different."

"A noble quest," he said. And interesting, considering that he was doing the same thing, in a way. On a surface level, at least. He had no interest in finding himself, what-ever that meant. But the idea of changing perceptions, that one grabbed him.

"Not really," she said. "Just a desire to be seen as some-thing other than a terminal dork."

"I can't imagine you being thought of as a...as that."

"Well, I was. Scrub off the makeup, add a ponytail...I re-vert right back. Actually, I don't think I'm evolved all that far beyond dork status—it's just that I have a better handle on confusing people by presenting a more polished appearance."

"Polished but flashy."

"Distract them with something shiny, right?"

In some ways he understood that philosophy, too. Bring a beautiful, bubbly date and people might not notice how much he hated being at public events. Might not notice how little he smiled.

"Right," he said, his eyes on her ring. He took her hand in his, ran his thumb over her smooth skin, to the gem that glittered on her finger. "This should do it," he said, looking up, meeting her gaze.

Her eyes were round, her lips parted slightly and he knew that he could lean in and kiss her and she would kiss him back. The desire to do it, the need, tightened his gut. They would have to do it in public eventually. It would be perfectly reasonable to give it a try now. To press his lips to that soft, pink mouth. To dip his tongue inside and find out if she tasted as explosive as she looked.

He turned away from her sharply, putting his focus back on his phone. He wouldn't kiss her. Not now. Not because he wanted to. Not because the desire, pumping hot and hard through his veins told him to. No, when there was a need for it, he would do it. Not before then.

He was in absolute control of his body, and his desires. Always. It would be no different with Paige. They were playing a game that bordered on dangerous, and that meant he had to be sure that he kept things tightly in line.

Paige cleared her throat. "Right. It certainly is...distracting."

"Yes," he said, clenching his teeth tight, "it is."

You can't have more champagne. You'll make a total ass of yourself.

She'd already rolled her ankle twice while walking around the lavishly decorated ballroom and had stumbled obviously, teetering sharply to the right thanks to her three-inch heels.

She wasn't exactly making the best appearance as Dante's brand-new fiancée.

But this had all happened so fast she hadn't had time to adjust. And that was one of the many reasons that alcohol felt slightly necessary.

The other was that moment in the car, just before they'd arrived, when Dante's dark eyes had been focused on her mouth. When heat and desire had spread through her, flushing her skin, making her heart race. When she'd looked like a total fool, drooling over a man who didn't have the slightest interest in her.

Yeah, there was that.

"Enjoying yourself, *cara mia*?" Dante appeared, holding two glasses of champagne. He offered her one, and she took it, in spite of herself.

"I'm not really sure," she said.

"You aren't sure?"

"No. I mean, I don't know anyone here but you so I'm basically just standing next to you smiling and no one is really talking to me and...my cheeks hurt."

"Your cheeks?"

"From the smiling."

"Ah." He frowned. "I must confess most of my dates aren't

here for conversation so I imagine the assumption has now been made about you."

"What are they here for?" she asked. The obvious, she imagined. The pleasure of having Dante later.

"For the publicity," he said, uprooting her previous assumption. "There will be several pictures of you, standing next to me and smiling, published in various places online and in print by tomorrow morning."

"So, women date you to get their picture in the paper?"

"I'm not really vain, but I don't think that's the only reason."

Paige's heart slammed hard against her breastbone as she thought of all the other reasons women might date Dante. Oh, yeah, she could see that for sure. "Well, I mean...I'm sure your sparkling wit and effusive personality also net you a few dinner engagements."

He laughed, a more genuine, rich laugh than she'd heard from him before. "I doubt it, somehow, but thank you for the confidence in me."

"Or course," she said. "It's the least I can do considering what you're doing for me."

"I'm getting something in return."

"You say that like you have to convince yourself you aren't being altruistic," she said, regretting the two glasses of champagne she'd already had, and the candor that came with them, the moment she said it.

"Because I never am."

"So can never be?"

"Mr. Romani, and your lovely fiancée!" They were interrupted by an older woman with a broad smile.

Dante inclined his head. "Nice to see you again, Catherine, and please, call me Dante."

"Dante, of course." Catherine began regaling Dante with stories of her country club, gossip, both personal and business related. She noticed that Dante managed to appear vaguely interested, his expression politely pleasant.

And yet she could see something behind his eyes. Calculation. She could almost see him filtering out the unimportant, retaining bits about failing businesses and mistresses who might cause trouble in someone's professional life.

Then he smiled, a smile that some might call warm, and bid the older woman goodbye.

"Who was that?" she asked.

"A friend of my…parents," he said, the word coming out in a few, halting syllables.

"Oh."

"I'll confess, I don't like these things, either," he said. "But, you do hear interesting information. It's worth it. So that about sums up my altruism, really. It's for charity, which is nice. But I get something out of it, too. Nothing is purely altruistic."

She thought of Ana, of how much joy Ana brought to her life. How much love and purpose. "I suppose not."

"Does the purity of motivation really matter anyway? As long as no one is hurt. As long as people are cared for?"

"I always imagined it did."

"Nobody gets points for good intentions."

"I suppose not." The champagne spoke for her again. "Does anyone hold bad intentions against you if you don't act on them?"

"Speaking of yourself, or of me?"

She shrugged. "Just curious if it works both ways."

"In my experience, intentions, and sometimes actions, don't really matter at all. What matters is what people think."

"Now that is true," she said, sighing heavily, thinking back to how people had perceived her in her home town. Of how the social worker perceived her and her situation.

He lifted his glass. "To reinvention," he said.

She lifted her glass in response but opted out of taking a sip. She needed to get her feet back on solid ground, needed to get her words back under control. And she really needed to get her thoughts in regards to Dante back under control.

"Perhaps when we're through with this you and I will both be totally different people," she said. "Or at least, in your case, people will think so."

A smile curved his lips. Not a friendly smile. One that was dangerous. And, though it really shouldn't have been, sexy. "Perhaps."

CHAPTER FIVE

PAIGE took her latte off the counter and waved to her favorite barista as she walked out the door of the coffee shop.

She paused and put her sunglasses on, taking a sip of her drink while admiring the afternoon light filtering through the palm trees. It was a perfect day. The light glinted on her new engagement ring and it put a slight dent in her moment of zen.

There was a flash to her left and she turned to look. It was not a little flare of afternoon light. There was a photographer, standing there, holding his camera up, not even trying to be subtle.

"Uh…could you not do that?" she asked.

"Ms. Harper?"

"What?"

"When are you and Dante Romani getting married?"

She clutched her sequined purse to her side and strode down the sidewalk, away from the man with the camera, her heart pounding. She turned back to look and saw that he was still there, snapping off shots casually. Like she was a monkey in a zoo.

Her purse vibrated and she reached inside, casting another glance behind her as she retrieved her phone and answered the call. "Hello?"

"Ms. Harper, this is Rebecca Addler with child services. I wanted to speak to you about your case."

She quickened her pace, heading back to the office building. Back to Ana. Back to Dante even. She could hide behind his broad chest. And she wasn't even ashamed for wanting to hide behind him right now.

"Right. Great to hear from you. What about the case?" she asked, scurrying through the revolving door to the Colson's corporate building and walking quickly to the elevators.

"We're going to have to interview your fiancé. He's going to be involved in the process, of course."

"Well, of course."

"And he'll be adopting Ana, as well."

Damn.

"So there will be paperwork for that," she finished.

Paige had overlooked that bit. She'd overlooked it completely. "Of course," she said, her throat dry. She took another sip of latte and scalded her mouth. She punched the up button on the wall and waited for an elevator.

She dashed inside as soon as the door opened.

"And we'll want to do a parent interview with him."

"Naturally. Dante will be delighted—" like Dante was ever delighted about anything "—to participate."

"We'll do a little meet-up this Friday if that works for you."

"Of course it does!" she said, far too brightly.

The elevator reached her floor, and she stood inside, waffling. Then she hit the button that would take her to Dante's floor and the door slid closed again.

She tapped her foot while she finalized the details of the appointment with Rebecca. She ended the phone call as quickly as possible and tapped her fingers on the wall, waiting for the elevator to stop. When it did, and the doors opened, she nearly ran out, past Trevor, and to Dante's office.

She didn't bother to knock.

"I just got my picture taken. Like...a hundred times by some photographer. And then Rebecca Addler called and said we need to start doing interviews as a couple. Oh, I just realized there will be a home study, and we'll have to start over and do it at your house because as far as everyone is con-

cerned that is where we'll be living. And you're going to adopt
Ana legally. Which is sort of...obvious but I didn't think of
it until now and...and I'm officially panicking a little bit."

"Don't," he said, standing from his position behind the
desk, his large, masculine hands planted palms down on the
pristine surface. He didn't even have the decency to look
surprised that she'd burst into his office. He just looked...
smooth and calm and unaffected as ever.

It was just unfair, because her cage was well and truly
rattled.

"Don't panic?"

"No. There's no need. When we divorce I'll sign custody
of Ana over to you. You have my word on that."

"Oh." She let out a breath she didn't know she'd been holding in a rush. "That does make me feel better."

"I thought it might."

"Then there's the home study."

"You and Ana should move in with me. Soon." That he
said with a kind of grim determination that let her know exactly what he thought of it.

"I can see you're completely thrilled at the idea."

"I value my own space," he said.

"Well, as you mentioned, it's a big house. I'm sure we
won't be on top of each other."

He lifted one dark brow, and horror crept over her as she
realized the double meaning of her words. As she pictured
just what it might be like to be on top of him.

Or to have him on top of her.

Her entire face heated, prickling awareness spreading over
her skin. Her heart was racing and she was...turned on. And
it was obvious. She was certain it was.

She was such a dork. A side effect of spending her school
years as the funny one. She didn't know how to be smooth;
she knew how to go for a joke. Another side effect of that
was that guys didn't flirt with her.

Well, that might have also been because of the time Michael Weston had tried to make out with her at a party and had ended up cutting his tongue on her braces. No one had wanted to kiss her after that. Kissing her became a running joke, and very firmly kept her in her place as school screwup.

Well, after that someone had made her *think* he wanted to kiss her, and more than that. It had all been a gag, of course. Thinking about that reduced the horror of the situation a little bit, because nothing, nothing in the history of the world, was quite as bad as meeting a guy under the bleachers after prom to…to…and having the popular kids standing by, waiting for just the right moment, waiting for the top of her prom dress to come down, for her "date" to pull her out from beneath the bleachers onto the field so they could throw eggs at her. And laugh. And take pictures of her humiliation for posterity.

Yes, that put a woman off dating for a while.

As a result, she wasn't great at handling men. Unless they were more like buddies. And Dante didn't feel like a buddy. Not even a little.

"You know what I mean," she said. "Don't look at me like that."

"Like what?"

"You know," she said, narrowing her eyes.

"As for the parent interview…" He neatly sidestepped the moment.

"What about it?"

"I don't see how it will be a problem."

"You may have to grow a personality between now and then."

"And you may want to tone yours down."

"Why because a fun-loving, smiley person might not make a good parent? Do I need to be a bit more dour?"

"Are you calling me…dour?" he asked.

"If the scowl fits."

"You're going to have to keep yourself from taking shots at me in the presence of the social worker. Actually, you should probably keep yourself from taking shots at me because I'm your boss."

She bit her lower lip. "Yeah. Okay, that could be…"

"And don't bite your lip like that." He leaned forward and extended his hand, putting his thumb on her chin, just beneath her mouth.

She slowly released her hold on her lip, her heart pounding heavily, butterflies taking flight in her stomach and crashing around, making her insides feel jittery.

She could only stare at him, at his incredibly handsome face, his dark, compelling eyes.

"I'll try not to," she said, not sure why she agreed with him. She should be annoyed that he was being so dictatorial, and yet she found she wasn't. But that could be because he was touching her, and men didn't make a habit of touching her.

It didn't mean she didn't want them to. It just hadn't really happened for her for many and varied reasons. A huge reason being she was too afraid to let a moment like that happen. Because she was afraid to acknowledge she wanted it, for fear of it all being a joke again.

"Good. You're also going to have to work on not blushing like a schoolgirl every time I get near you."

"I don't blush." She could feel the heat creeping into her face, calling her bluff.

"You blush more than any woman I've ever seen."

"I'm very pale. It's hard to hide when you have no pigment to disguise it."

"I imagine," he said. "Even so, if we were truly engaged we would be well past the point where I could make you blush with just the casual brush of my hands. Unless…" he said, rounding the desk, coming to stand near her. "Unless you were thinking of all the things my hands have done for you."

His voice changed, became rougher, more ragged. Something in his expression changed, too. Hardened. Never, ever, ever had a man looked at her like that before. Not even close.

She wanted to say something to defuse the tension. Something funny, or random, something to break the spell. But she couldn't. A part of her didn't want to. She wanted to stand there, and have Dante Romani look at her like she was the most fascinating thing he'd ever seen. She wanted to get closer to him, see if he was as hot as he looked. To see if the fire smoldering in his eyes would burn her.

"I...suppose that could be a possibility." She looked down, trying to catch her breath. But her eyes connected with his hands, and that did not help her regulate her breathing. "Subtext, right? Like when you're acting? You make sure that even your thoughts match those of your character. And...stuff."

"Something like that," he said.

Of course to really have good subtext she would have to know exactly what he could do with his hands, and frankly, some of that information was a little hazy for her. And she was in no position to change it. Not now, not with him. And, given that she was going to be single mother of a small child for quite a few years, maybe not anytime soon.

That had never really been her plan. But she'd been too afraid to put herself out there after the way she'd been treated. Too afraid of rejection.

Dante picked up his phone and dialed a number. "Trevor, I need you to hire some movers. Send them to Paige's apartment. The address is on file. Personal items only, no furniture, all of the baby supplies. It needs to be done by the end of the day." He hit the end button on the phone and put it back in the holder on his desk.

"Did you just...evict me?"

"You'll keep the apartment, for later. I assume that's the place you'll go back to."

"Yeah, I think I'll need my home. But what's going to happen with it in the meantime?"

"There's no reason to do anything with the apartment. I can handle the rent for you for the duration of your stay at my home."

"I pay the rent. I'm not having trouble with the rent—there's no reason for you to pay it for me!"

He shrugged. "But I can, so I don't see why it's an issue."

"Because *I* can," she said.

"Don't be stubborn."

"Me? You're telling me not to be stubborn? That is funny, Dante, real funny."

"This ruse really ought to be easy. In fact, they may assume we've been married for twenty years given the way you argue with me."

"I argue with you? Hmph."

"Yes, you do. Just like that."

"Well, I'm annoyed with you."

"Then you had better get un-annoyed, *cara*. Remember, this whole thing is of your making. I never would have sought you out." His words made her flinch internally. "I will take advantage of the situation, yes, but I would not have sought you out. You're completely unsuitable, obviously, and if I had felt the need for a wife pressing I would have one already."

Stupidly, a little pang of hurt hit her square in the chest, knocking the wind out of her, making her eyes sting. "I'm… unsuitable? Wh-why?"

She shouldn't have asked why. Not when she really didn't want to hear it all.

"Am I suitable to you?" he asked, his tone incredulous.

"No," she said. "No, you're rude. And obnoxious. And you don't know how to laugh."

He took a step toward her, his dark eyes intent on hers. "And you are disorganized and scattered."

"I must not be too bad since you keep me on here. Clearly I know how to do my job."

"As do hundreds of my employees, but that does not mean they would make a good spouse for me."

She took a step toward him, tossing her hair back over her shoulders. "I'm sure they feel the same way about you."

He reached out his hand and took a lock of her hair, her

pink hair, between his thumb and forefinger. "I would clearly never become involved with a woman who has pink hair."

She leaned in, up on her tiptoes, trying to make herself eye level with him. "And I would never become involved with a man who's more starched than his shirt collar."

He reached out and wrapped his arm around her waist, drawing her up against his hard body. She squeaked as her breasts came up against the muscular wall of his chest. "You think I'm too serious, is that it?" She nodded mutely, no words coming to her. "That I don't know how to have fun." His fingers flexed against her back, sending little pops of sensation from the point of contact all throughout her body.

"Yes," she managed, heat flooding her.

He dipped his head so that his lips were nearly touching her cheek, his breath hot on her skin. "I think I might surprise you."

She was trembling, actually trembling, and in danger of having a knee-buckling experience. No man had ever held her like this before. With such purpose, with such strength. No man had ever made her feel so wanted. No man had ever made her want to arch against him, press her breasts harder into his body.

And most especially, no man had made her want to kiss him while she was angry at him.

But here she was, quivering with the need to touch Dante, even while thinking murderous thoughts about him and his autocratic behavior.

Dante released her suddenly and she stumbled back, trying hard to catch her breath. She looked at him, searched his face for some sign of what he was thinking. To try to figure out if he was as affected, as shaken, as she was.

But he wasn't. He was just standing there, his hair smooth, his suit crisp, as though he had never taken her into his arms. As though he hadn't just held her so close she could feel his heart beating, hard and heavy against her chest.

"You had better figure out a way to forgive me," he said.

And that was when she realized that he was affected. Because he might look as smooth as ever, but his voice was rough, his shredded control evident in each word he spoke. "Because at the end of the day, you're coming home with me."

CHAPTER SIX

DANTE'S home was his most prized possession. The lawn was immaculate, cut perfectly and kept in top condition by his team of groundskeepers.

The house itself was a triumph of architecture. Clean lines, an open design, windows that made the most of the ocean view. The interior was white, the carpets, the walls, the furniture. Evidence of how orderly it was.

Evidence of the control he now held over his life.

And as Paige, with her glittery high heels, walked over the threshold, carrying a bright-eyed baby girl with drool running down her chin, he felt a pang of absolute dread hit him in the gut.

There was nothing orderly about either of them, and he could feel the hard-won control of his surroundings slipping away from him.

"This is…" Paige looked around, her mouth open, her blue eyes round. "This is incredible. Gorgeous. I don't… I've never seen anything like it."

"I had it built five years ago, shortly after the control of Colson's passed to me."

"I'm thinking the social worker will like this place better than she liked mine."

"Probably," he said, thinking of her cluttered little apartment. "I apologize for my lack of boxed wine. I suppose something from the cellar with have to do."

"Now, now, nobody likes a show-off."

"That depends on what they're being shown."

"Heh. No, it depends on how much money and power the show-off possesses, and then the person will pretend to be suitably impressed based on how much they figure ingratiating themselves will help them out."

"So you think my admirers are merely out to use me for my wealth and fame?"

She shrugged. "Not so far-fetched, is it?"

"You're not very good for my ego, Paige, as you seem to think no one would suffer my company without heavy compensation."

"That's not what I meant. Oh...pfft. I like your house—that's the important thing right now."

"I assume the location of your bedrooms are important, as well?"

"Bedrooms?"

"Ana will have a nursery. I called my housekeeper earlier and ensured that all of her things have been put in there."

"A nursery?"

He let out an exasperated sigh. "Did you think I would cram you both in the basement to keep you out of the way?"

"Well, I didn't know. I didn't... We really need to discuss this more."

"I agree, which is why we're having dinner together later."

"Oh."

"Here, so you don't need to worry about a babysitter. Now come with me." He started up the stairs and down the hall. He could hear Paige's footsteps behind him, slow and methodical. He turned and saw that she was practically getting whiplash. "What is it?"

"Your art!" she said.

"What about it?"

"It's so beautiful. And it really stands out in the white space. You have fabulous taste."

"Fabulous? Rarely am I accused of being fabulous."

"Well, in this instance, you are. I'm going to have to take the time to study it all later."

"So, you like art?"

She smiled and her entire face brightened, her blue eyes glittering. "Love it. I'm not just into dressing windows. I paint, too. Well, I started with painting. And some sculpture. It was about the only thing that held my attention in school. Unfortunately, one cannot graduate with art credits alone."

"I would guess not." The enthusiasm she felt for the subject, for the paintings—paintings he hardly looked at anymore—was fascinating. She was so different than most of the people he knew. She was open. She wore her passion all over her, for anyone to read. Not just her passion, her anger, her happiness. Everything was just laid bare with her.

And she evoked something in him. Emotions, things he hadn't felt in longer than he could remember. As a result, he'd made a mistake in his office earlier, and he didn't make mistakes.

But she'd been standing there, all challenge and fire, angry as hell. And she'd made him angry. More than that, she'd tempted him. He hadn't been able to stop himself from walking forward, from wrapping his arm around her and drawing her body against his.

She challenged him. No one challenged him. But she did. And she picked at his control, pushing and pushing until he'd been unable to do anything but push back.

He didn't like it. Emotion was destructive. Painful. But he wouldn't give in to it. What he hadn't lost the day his mother died had been drained from him over the course of eight years in foster care.

Now, he doubted there was even enough in him to cause problems, even if he wanted it to. No, what had come over him in his office was lust. Pure and simple. Normally, that wasn't a problem for him, but he was only a man, so it wasn't too surprising.

Paige had the added benefit of being forbidden fruit, another thing that had never appealed to him before, but he could certainly understand why it might.

"Ana's room is here," he said, redirecting his thoughts, indicating a door on the left. As he pushed it open, a strange flash of anxiety ran through him. It was unfamiliar. Completely different than it had been that morning when he'd left for work. It gave him a strange sense of being back in his childhood. Opening the door to a new bedroom for the first time, seeing what was there.

Whether it would be spare, or crowded. Clean or dirty. Nothing that belonged to him.

The space that had been organized for Ana was immaculate.

Plain white walls and a double bed had been replaced with an ornate, dark wood crib with pink bedding and a mobile hanging over it. There was a rocking chair, a matching dresser and a closet filled with pink clothes.

"Oh." Behind him Paige made a little noise. Then she brushed past him and into the room. "Ana, look. It's your very own room."

His chest seized up tight, his breath locking in his lungs. The light in Paige's eyes as she presented Ana with a space that belonged to her was...he had never seen anything like it. All of Paige's unruly enthusiasm was, in this moment, focused on her daughter.

How anyone could doubt that she would be a good mother was beyond him. It was hard for him to remember his birth mother, hard because thinking about her always dredged up other memories that he wanted to keep firmly locked behind a closed door in his mind.

Mary Colson, his adoptive mother, had been a firm and constant presence. Both she and Don had invested in him, into his education, into guiding him, putting him on a path that would lead to success. He was grateful to them, and their distant, tough sort of parenting had been ideal for him.

But for a moment, he wondered if anyone had ever looked at him the way Paige was looking at Ana.

It didn't matter. He closed the door on the yawning, empty well inside of him. He wasn't a child. He didn't need obvious displays of emotion. Far from it, he avoided them if at all possible. And being around Paige didn't seem to allow for that. She was constant bubbling energy, and emotion. And glitter.

"Thank you," she said, her blue eyes bright.

"Don't thank me," he said, trying to find some way to loosen the knot in his chest. "You're here under false pretenses, due to a situation of your own making. And it's hardly permanent, so don't get too attached."

She blinked, a flash of genuine pain visible on her face. So open. So real. Did the woman have no sense? Had she no defenses at all? "Okay, I...I mean I know that, but this is beautiful and I just got really excited and I didn't mean anything by it." All of her words ran together, coming faster as she rambled, the tension she was feeling palpable. She projected her feelings. So strongly he felt like he was being hit with a wall.

"Relax, Paige," he said. "Take a breath."

She snapped her mouth closed, her eyes still pooling with confused emotion.

"I'm sorry," he said, the word foreign on his tongue.

Almost instantly, the tension left her, her face brightening. "It's awkward. For everyone. I know. I'm not picking out china patterns or anything, I'm just...making the best of things. Making the best of living in a mansion by the sea, which, I admit, is not so hard."

"You may not be so optimistic when you hear what I have to say next," he said.

"You're putting me on a hide-a-bed. No, my window has an ocean view, but the beach is a nude beach. Or maybe..."

"You're going to have to at least appear to be sharing a room with me."

"Say what?"

"Come now, Paige, are you so naive? If we've moved in together, we'll obviously be sharing a room. A bed."

Paige bit her bottom lip. "I don't know about that. What about good, traditional values?"

"Does anyone have them these days?"

"My social worker, it seems. Since she was so concerned about Ana having a mom and dad."

"Which means she needs to be confident that that is indeed what Ana is getting. And my staff needs to believe it, as well. The last thing I need is for someone to slip up and make a comment that winds up in the paper. I'm not being dragged into a public farce. A private farce, it seems, is unavoidable, but I will not be humiliated in a public forum."

"That's not my intent," she said. "But hey, as long as I don't actually have to sleep with you, I'm okay with having to dig through your closet to find my clothes."

He wasn't. He'd never lived with a woman before, had never had feminine things mingling in with his suits. His space was highly prized and this element of their arrangement didn't sit well with him.

But while she was comfortable with her things being put anywhere, there was clearly one area that made her uncomfortable. And he had the uncontrollable urge to push at her, just a little.

"You're the first woman I've ever encountered who was so opposed to sleeping with me she had to remark on it every couple of days."

He was rewarded by the flood of color that bled into her cheeks. "That's not... I'm just clarifying..."

"One might think," he said, taking a step closer to her, "that you protest too much."

She pulled Ana in tighter to her chest, a tiny, living shield. "Hey now, that is not true. I protest just enough for a woman who isn't interested in having a...a fling with a playboy."

"Playboy," he said. "Such a strange label, and not one I've ever felt applied to me."

"You change lovers often enough."

"The dates I go to events with are not my lovers. I am very discreet with my lovers. And selective."

She cleared her throat. "Well, then, I doubt I have anything to worry about. If you're as selective as you say, I mean."

Paige felt like melting beneath Dante's intense, dark gaze. She didn't know what had possessed her to bait him like that. To tempt him to say something derogatory about her appeal. She was aware of how far short she fell when it came to sexual allure.

The problem was, it wasn't looks, not specifically. It wasn't the way she dressed. She'd actually managed to score dates since moving to San Diego; it was just that…when they got that serious look, like they might miss her, she sort of freaked out. The idea of failing again, with someone new, was too painful. The thought of wanting someone who wouldn't really end up wanting her…she hadn't been willing to take the risk.

Which was why she really hadn't bothered with dates for a long time. Getting herself sorted out was her top priority after all. Finding her way. And anyway, she didn't need a hundred guys. She only needed the one right guy. And she was certain that one right guy would look nothing like Dante Romani.

Which was fine. Looks weren't everything after all. The guy didn't have to have a square jaw, and golden skin. Or a broad chest with incredible muscles that could not be hidden by the dress shirts he wore. He didn't have to look like the essence of temptation wrapped in a custom suit. No. There were much more important things than that.

Like…way more.

She was sure of it.

"Is that what you think?" he asked.

Something in his eyes changed, the look becoming hungry, wild almost, as far from cool, calm, stuffed shirt Dante Romani as she could possibly imagine.

"I…obviously," she said, her throat suddenly dry.

"What is obvious about it?" he asked.

"I'm…I'm…"

"Attractive," he said.

She blinked. "Even with the pink stripe?"

"It's growing on me."

"Maybe I *will* get it colored over next time. In that case."

"You just like to be difficult."

She shrugged. "I'm a contrary beast, on occasion, I admit it." She was doing it again, deflecting with humor, so he couldn't see how much it had meant for him to call her attractive.

"I like a challenge."

"I'm not a challenge," she said, nerves skittering through her, making her feel shaky and off-kilter.

"You aren't?"

"No. That makes it sound like I'm some sort of a…a game and I don't like that. I don't play games. What you see is what you get."

"I've noticed. But I didn't mean that I intended to play a game with you."

"You didn't?"

He shook his head, his dark eyes intent on hers. "I don't play."

She tried to swallow again. Her throat felt like it was coated in sand. "Right. Neither do I."

He chuckled, dark and rich like chocolate. "I got the impression that you did very little besides playing."

She looked down at the top of Ana's fuzzy head. "And where did you get that idea? Between working for Colson's and taking care of Ana, I don't have a lot of playtime."

He frowned. "I suppose that's true. But it's more the way you are. The things you say. You're…happy."

She laughed, the sound bursting from her with no decorum or volume control, as always. "I guess so. I mean, there's plenty of crap I'm unhappy about. Like losing my best friend and having to contend with the adoption stuff. But I suppose…I mean in general I suppose that's true." She studied Dante's face for a moment, the lines that feathered out from the corners of his eyes, the brackets by his mouth. "Are you happy?"

He shrugged. "I'm not really sure what that means. I'm content."

"Content," she repeated. She smoothed her hands over Ana's back and a rush of love, or pure joy and pain filled her. "How can that be enough?" It wasn't for her. Not now. It never would be again.

"Because emotion, strong emotion, is dangerous," he said. "You don't seem to realize that yet, Paige. But that's the truth of it." His voice was rough. Savage, almost. And coming from Dante, who was always smooth, and never ruffled, it meant something. It reached down deep inside of her and twisted her stomach.

"Was it the truth for you?"

"It's just true," he said. "If emotions control you, you have no control over yourself. In my mind, that's unacceptable. Now come, and I'll show you to your room."

CHAPTER SEVEN

AFTER you put Ana to bed, come down to the dining room for dinner.

Paige touched the note Dante had left her earlier. A note. Who wrote a note? She'd have to introduce the man to the mighty power of the text message. Or, better still, making human contact when you lived in the same house as someone.

She touched one of the letters on the paper. He'd pressed too hard on his pen, made dents, each letter precise and perfect, gone over two or three times she guessed. Dante didn't do spontaneous very well, that was for sure.

Well, she supposed their arrangement fell under spontaneous, but then, even when he'd had that headline sprung on him he hadn't acted with any sense of wild abandon. It had been with frightening calm, and complete confidence in the fact that he'd made the right decision.

Whereas, she, after blurting out the idiot untruth to Rebecca, had eaten a pint of ice cream and spent the night beating her head against the arm of her couch.

Decisive wasn't really her thing. She needed to start getting there, though. She had a baby. A baby that would grow, and who would need a mother who could stand strong in decisions and discipline and…stuff.

The idea of it made her a little anxious. But for now, it was all about loving her. And that she had down just fine.

At least her room was nice. And yeah, all her clothes and

her toiletries were in Dante's room, but she'd managed to get her dress for dinner and her makeup essentials over to her room without running into him. Which suited her fine. She'd been feeling a little rumpled and frumpy after what had been a very long day.

But a shower and a sparkly minidress had done a lot to fix the way she felt. Her newfound sense of flashy style was something she'd acquired on arrival in San Diego, and it had done wonders for the way she felt about herself. About the outside of herself, anyway.

She leaned into the mirror and swiped her lipstick over her bottom lip, painting it with a streak of fuchsia, then spreading it evenly. She smiled. She felt better when she was bright. Like showing the world her mood, so that she had to bring herself up to match it.

She let out a long breath and opened her bedroom door, padding quietly down the hall to Ana's room first, to make sure she was sleeping soundly, then continued to the stairs. She took the stairs two at a time, anxious now to hear what Dante would say.

To see if he would tease her again. Flirt with her? No, he wouldn't flirt with her. There was no reason for that.

She tripped on the last step, her focus splintered over her thoughts.

"Careful."

She looked up and her heart slammed hard against her breast. Dante was standing in the doorway of the dining room, his eyes on her. On her nearly falling on her face. He, on the other hand, looked immaculate as always. Perfectly pressed in a crisp white shirt that was open at the collar, showing a faint shadow of chest hair that she couldn't help but notice, and black slacks that showed off his trim waist and powerful thighs.

Since when had she ever noticed a man's thighs? What was he doing to her?

"I like to make an entrance," she said, doing a very lopsided curtsy in an attempt to defuse the tension. All she really succeeded in doing was making herself look like a bit of an ass. That seemed to be her specialty. But it didn't matter really. She just kept smiling. If she didn't care, no one else seemed to. No one else seemed to notice how hard things were, how awkward she felt, if she didn't.

She straightened and smiled, hoping she didn't blush.

"You certainly do that." He walked toward her, the easy grace in his movements filling her with one part envy and nine parts desire. He really was gorgeous.

"Ha. Yeah. My blessing and my curse."

He put his hand on her lower back and heat fired through her from that point to the rest of her body. He propelled her forward into the dining room and she was afraid she might wobble again. Not because she was that big of a klutz, not usually, but because his touch was making her limbs feel rubbery.

She sucked in a breath when she saw the table. It was laid out special—gorgeous platters with appetizers and there were candles. It was very real, suddenly. Like an actual date, which she knew it wasn't.

And she shouldn't let it make her feel any kind of pressure. He wasn't interested in her that way, and that was fine with her. She didn't have the time or inclination for it.

"This looks great," she said, too brightly.

He pulled her chair out for her and looked at her, waiting for her. She just stared.

"Would you like to sit down?" he asked.

"Oh, uh...yes. I'm not used to men pulling my chair out for me."

"Then you need to associate with better men."

"Or maybe find men to associate with in general."

"I imagine your dating life is somewhat hobbled by recent developments."

"Yeah, recent developments. That's what's hobbled my dating life." She sat down and he abandoned his post at her chair and went to sit across from her. She took a salmon roll off the platter and put it onto her plate, her stomach growling, reminding her it was late for dinner. "So," she said, "you want to talk?"

"We need to talk. I'm not sure I particularly want to talk. But we need a plan. If we're going to be a couple, to both child services and the media we need to know about each other."

"And how do you propose we get to know each other?" she asked, taking a bite of the sushi.

"I'm not proposing we get to know each other. I'm proposing we learn things about each other. The two are different."

"Less involved, I suppose," she said.

"Much." He took a roll off the platter with a pair of chopsticks. Effortless for him, as ever. "Where are you from?"

"Silver Creek. Oregon. Small, bit of a nothing town. Everyone knows your business. Everyone knows you. The entire population is kind of like your extended family."

"Which is why you moved."

"Yes. To somewhere that didn't have people with...expectations." Expectations of her failure. Of her continuing to drift through life without a goal, without any success. "And you, where are you from?"

"Rome originally. Then moved to Los Angeles. And then...when my mother died," he said, his voice too smooth, too controlled, as if he was saying words he'd rehearsed to perfection, "I went into foster care. I spent a few years with different families before the Colsons adopted me at fourteen."

"I could have found all that out by reading a bio online somewhere."

"But had you read one?"

"No."

"So, I still had to tell you."

"Fine, you did. What else do I need to know?" she asked.

He slid two covered plates over from the edge of the table and placed one in front of her, and one in front of himself. She uncovered it and took a moment to appreciate the tantalizing look and smell of the fish dish before directing her focus back to Dante.

"My sign?" he asked, his tone dry.

She laughed. "I don't even know my own sign. I don't pay attention to that stuff."

"That surprises me—you seem like you would."

"Why?"

"Because you're very…free-spirited. And you're an artist."

"I see. Well, sorry to disappoint you. What's your favorite color?"

"I don't have one."

"That's stupid. Everyone has a favorite color."

He arched one dark eyebrow. "Did you just call me stupid?"

"No. Your lack of favorite color is stupid."

"Fine, what's yours?"

"Well, I'm an artist, so I have a close relationship with color. I like cool colors—they're very calming. And of course warm colors are quite passionate. So I have to say my favorite color is…glitter."

He laughed and she felt a small tug of gratification that she's managed to pull an expression of humor out of him. "That isn't a color."

"Sure it is. I'm an expert. I don't question you about merchandising and advertising and everything else you have a hand in. Siblings?" she asked.

"No," he said. "You?"

"Two. My sister is a pediatrician and my brother is a second-string quarterback for the Seahawks. Impressive, I know."

"Very. So how did you get into art?"

She fought off the sting of embarrassment that always came when she had to talk about Jack and Emma. It wasn't fair, really. They deserved their success. They earned it. They had talent, and they worked hard.

They didn't deserve for her to make it about her. Still, it

was never fun to talk about. But talking about it was better than living in a town where everyone knew that you were, without question, the big letdown of your family.

"I've always been interested in it. Started drawing and painting really young."

"Did you go to school for it?"

"No." She shook her head, kept her tone light. No big deal. It was no big deal. "I never really liked school. Just wasn't my thing."

"And what did your parents think of that?"

"Would you like me to lie down on the couch before you continue?"

"Just a question."

"Well, uh…they've never been that impressed with my interests. My grades in school were bad, and they were spending a lot of money sending Jack and Emma to school already, even with the help of scholarships and…and they didn't want to pay to send me too when they knew I wouldn't apply myself. So the not going to school was a mutual decision."

She could feel Dante's dark gaze boring into her. "A mutual decision?"

She shrugged. "I mean, I might have gone if they…"

"But they wouldn't."

"No."

"Should we tell your parents about the wedding?"

The subject change threw her for a moment. "Oh, it's… No, probably not. It's not like it will be huge news outside of our circle here. Your circle here, I should say and anyway… they won't really approve of the whole thing with Ana." An understatement. She could just hear her mother's skepticism.

Do you think you can handle it, Paige? Filled with concern, and a bit of condescension.

But she could handle it. She was sure she could. She was almost completely sure. Again, the bigness of it all threatened to swamp her completely. She couldn't remember the last time she'd really wanted something. The last time succeeding had been so important, if it ever had been.

It was so much easier to just not care. But with Ana, she couldn't.

"They don't approve of you adopting?" he asked.

She shrugged and put her focus back on her food. "I haven't talked to them about it, but I figure if I save it until everything is final I can spare everyone a lot of angst. It still might not work out." Her throat tightened, terror wrapping icy fingers around her neck.

"It will," he said, total confidence in his tone. "We have the media involved which, now that I think of it, is very likely going to work in your favor. I doubt social services want reports out about how they denied an adoption to a child's lifelong, primary caregiver."

"You may have a point. I have to ask, though, what's really in it for you? Because I don't have any guarantee that you won't back out. I know you talked about easing business deals but clearly you make deals just fine without me, so I can't fathom why it would suddenly be important."

He shrugged one shoulder. "I have opportunistic tendencies. This opportunity presented itself and I decided to follow it to its conclusion. There were two options in this situation— do what was expected of me, accept the negative press. Or, try to change things."

"And that's all? Because truly, with that as your only motivation, I'm not really filled with comfort and warm fuzzies."

His gaze sharpened, his dark eyes intense. "It's important for you to know something. When I say I will do something, I do. There is no going back."

He said it with such purpose, such unequivocal certainly that she couldn't help but believe him.

"You didn't have to do this," she said. It was the truth. She was the one in the stranglehold. She was the one who was in a situation that was too big for her, nothing unusual there. She was the one who needed help.

But instead of giving up, like she usually did, she'd done whatever she'd had to in order to secure her success. Unfortunately, that had meant lying. It had meant dragging Dante into the situation, and she really did sort of feel bad about that.

"I am doing it. I made the decision. I won't change my mind."

"But is the media thing…that's all you want?" she asked. Seriously, it was a stupid question because she didn't exactly have anything to give him if changing his image in the press wasn't enough.

He put his fork down, and took in a deep breath, his expression one of barely contained annoyance. "I have been the target of malicious rumor and speculation by the media since I was fourteen years old. I came onto the stage a villain. I thought it might be interesting to see if I could end up a hero."

There was no real venom in his words, none of the emotion that was so easy for her to think should be there. That the media had been attacking him since he was a young teenager seemed unforgivable. But he just said it like it was an interesting fact. And he talked about changing public perception as if it were no more than a fascinating experiment.

"What did they…say about you?"

"That I had somehow tricked the Colsons into adopting me. That I was holding something over their heads, that I was a plant for the Mafia—racially motivated attacks are always nice. That I might murder the poor, trusting older couple in their beds."

He spoke so casually, without inflection. Cold horror settled in her stomach, making her shiver. He continued. "Some thought Don Colson had 'imported' me because I was some sort of financial genius and he lacked an heir."

"But you knew the truth," she said, her heart tightening, aching for him. Things with her family were hard, and sometimes she felt like she didn't belong, but she didn't have the media weighing in on it.

He paused for a moment. "That's the thing. Paige, I don't

know the truth. Why they would take me in is somewhat beyond me. A fourteen-year-old boy with no people skills and
no inclination to find any. But I was smart," he said, as if
trying to reason it out. "I did well in school."

Oh, good, he was a genius, too.

"I'm sure it was more than that," she said. Because she
really needed to believe that getting good grades in school
wasn't the deciding factor on a person's value. Otherwise
she was sunk.

"Perhaps. I'll have to ask them sometimes."

"You never have?"

"It doesn't matter."

"But it does."

"No," he said, his voice hard, "it doesn't. They gave me
a future, the best education possible, the best job opportunity possible. They gave me the means to support myself."
He chuckled. "That might be an understatement. They gave
me the means to thrive. They owe me nothing. No explanation. No frilly words. I don't need them. I have everything I
need. And I think you and I have everything we need, too."

He stood from the table, his food less than half-finished.
"I'll see you in the morning. We'll all drive to work together.
It would look wrong to go separately."

She nodded and watched him walk out of the room. She
picked up her fork and started eating again. She wasn't going
to go to bed starving just because he'd decided to get upset
about something and leave.

And he was upset. For all that he'd stayed calm, she could
tell that the conversation had disturbed him.

There was so much more to her poker-faced boss. Finding out just what lay beneath the surface should be the fur-
thest thing from her mind. It didn't matter. Nothing mattered
but Ana.

But it was Dante dominating her thoughts tonight. She
sighed and tried to focus on her dinner, and not think so much

about the deep, overwhelming darkness that she'd glimpsed in his normally expressionless eyes.

Dante unbuttoned his shirt and took a hanger out of his closet. He put it on the hanger and buttoned the top few buttons, then put it in its place in the closet

He moved his hand to his belt buckle, then paused for a moment. He walked into his en suite bathroom and braced his hands on the vanity countertop, looking at his reflection in the mirror.

He didn't look at himself often. He didn't see much point in it. But he did now. And he wondered what other people saw.

He chuckled, the sound bitter, hollow in the empty room, and turned the sink on, running cold water onto his hand, splashing it onto his face. He knew what people thought about him. They wrote it in on society blogs and people, people from all over, were able to leave comments with their explicit opinions.

Sexy, but dead behind the eyes.

Amoral.

Italian bastard.

Impostor.

Yes, he knew what people thought of him. How they saw him. And he knew that it didn't matter. Not because he was so at peace with who he was, but because he genuinely didn't care.

A man makes his own destiny. If he is in control of himself, he can control everything around him.

Words from Don Colson when he'd first come to live with them. From the man he thought of as his father. The man he'd never felt worthy of calling father. It was what made him strive to be worthy. The Colsons were the only people who'd inspired that feeling in him.

Control was the key. It was what put him on Don Colson's side. And not on the side of his real father. The man who'd spilled his mother's blood. The man whose blood ran through his veins.

He shut off the water and turned, walking back into his room. His bedroom door opened and Paige stopped short, one foot in the room, a sharp squeak escaping her lips.

"I thought you were…that is…you didn't say anything when I knocked, and my pj's are in here. I'll…come back."

It took him a moment to realize that her wide eyes were glued to his bare chest. It gave him a strange sense of satisfaction to know that, in spite of her constant reminders that she didn't want to sleep with him, she wasn't immune to him.

Something that shouldn't matter.

"No need. Find your pajamas," he said. "Don't mind me."

"Right," she said, sliding into the room and moving quickly to the closet. She opened it and walked in. He watched her rummaging in the corner that had been designated for her clothing. He would have to ask his housekeeper to lay things out more nicely for her. His closet was huge, and his clothes always well spaced out so he could see what he had. There was no harm in crowding things in a little bit for Paige's sake.

Although, just when the idea of giving her some substantial room in his home had stopped bothering him, he wasn't sure. Maybe, *stopped bothering him* wasn't the right way to put it. More that it didn't make his eye twitch.

"Got them." She emerged a moment later, clutching a pair of flannel pants and a white T-shirt to her chest. "So I'll go."

He found that he was reluctant to let her leave. If she left, he would be alone with his thoughts, and tonight, his thoughts were on a dangerous path.

"Those don't look like I imagined they might," he said, extending his hand, taking the flannel between his thumb and forefinger.

"No?" she asked. He noticed that her chest pitched sharply, in time with a sudden breath. That his drawing nearer to her was making her nervous. That he was right in his earlier assessment of her. She wasn't immune to him.

"No," he said. "Something diaphanous and flowing, I thought. Something with glitter."

"And slippers with heels and feathers?" she asked, her voice thin and shaky.

"Also a tiara." He took a step closer to her, heat firing in his blood. He was thinking too much tonight and being near her made him feel less like thinking, and more like acting.

He lifted his hands and brushed his finger along her cheekbone. Her mouth dropped open, her lush lips forming an O. Oh, yes, this was simpler.

He slid his hand around, cupping her head, his thumb stroking her face still. "Even so, this has a certain appeal to it. As does the dress you have on now."

"D-Dante..."

"If we are going to be a couple, do couple interviews and things like that, you will have to look comfortable with me touching you."

"I'm comfortable," she said, the high pitch of her voice proving her a liar.

He wasn't comfortable, either. He was shaking, he was hard as hell and he couldn't fight the need that was coursing through him, not anymore. He had seen her, he had wanted her. Wondered what it would be like to taste all that color and light. To absorb it into himself.

But he had denied himself. No more.

Without thought for consequence, without even trying to gentle his movements or ask her if she was all right, he leaned in and pressed his lips to hers. She was so warm. So alive. Her breath filled him, the soft sound of shock she made when he slid his tongue over the seam of her mouth, made his stomach twist.

Keeping one hand on the back of her head, he curved his other arm around her waist and pulled her to him. Her arms were pinned between them, still clutching her pajamas, keeping him from feeling her body against his.

He reached between them and tugged the clothes from her

hands, scattering them over the bedroom floor. She pressed her hands flat against his bare chest, her palms warm, her touch sending a shock of heat and fire through him.

He traced her bottom lip with his tongue and she opened to him, offering him entry into her mouth. He felt like drowning in her. Like losing himself completely.

He didn't realize he'd starting moving until Paige's back came up against his bedroom wall. She was pinned between the hard surface and him, her breasts pressing into his chest. So he deepened the kiss. Took more. Demanded more.

Her hands were still pressed tight against his chest and for a moment, he thought she might be pushing him away.

No. No, he needed more. He continued to kiss her, devouring her, until she relaxed against him, until her hands crept upward, fingers curling around his neck, clinging to him.

Yes.

His heart was pounding, sweat beading over his skin. She dug her fingernails into his neck, holding on to him tightly, pressing in closer so that his heavy length was resting against her stomach.

There was no room for rational thought. There was no thought at all. Not beyond the next hot, wet slide of her tongue on his. Not beyond the next gasp of pleasure that came from her lips. There was nothing but bright lights bursting behind his closed eyes, and a pounding need to take her, join himself to her. Go deep inside. So deep he would lose himself completely.

It would be the easiest thing to push her dress up, tug her panties down, free his aching erection and push inside her tight, wet body. Find solace in her release, and in his. To let go.

He jerked back, his heart thundering, his body protesting. This was not how he operated. Not why he had sex. Not how he allowed himself to live. He couldn't allow it. Not ever.

He would never give in to that creeping darkness inside

of himself. To the monster that lived in him. The thing that he hated most.

"I'm sorry," he said, his words clipped.

She blinked. "Why?"

"It shouldn't have happened," he bit out. It was inexcusable. The loss of control. The desperation he'd felt. To use her as a salve for his wounds. To let go of everything completely.

"I see," she said. She bent down and started collecting her clothes, her movements jerky, awkward. She seemed angry, upset.

"You think it was a good idea?" he asked, frustration pounding his temples, arousal pounding in his groin.

"What? Oh…it's just…" She stood up. "Whatever." She waved her hand in dismissal. "It was a kiss. It's not like it was anything serious. No big deal. Lips. Tongue. Not a big…I'm gonna go now." She sidestepped out of the room and closed the door behind her.

Dante wrenched his belt off and threw it on the ground, stalking into his bathroom and turning the shower on cold. He dropped his pants and underwear and stepped beneath the spray. He let the icy water roll over him, making him shiver, his body shaking from the inside out. It wasn't about cooling the heat in his body. He was paying penance for losing his control.

It would not happen again.

Paige leaned against her bedroom door, her heart sill pounding heavily, her lips still burning. Just a kiss? No big deal? She was getting good at lying.

She'd never been kissed like that, by a man like him, in her life.

And of course, the first words out of his mouth had been that it was a mistake. Of course it had been. How could it be anything else? A man like him would not want to kiss a woman like her. Not really.

Sometimes she felt like she was changing. Finding out who

she was apart from the labels she'd been given at home, back in high school. Tonight, she felt like she'd reverted. Back to the painfully awkward girl she'd been.

The one she still was beneath the makeup and sequins.

She changed into her pajamas as quickly as possible and tried to ignore just how conscious she was of the fabric sliding against her skin. Of how sensitive she felt. He'd lit her skin on fire, made her feel like she was burning from the inside out.

The memory of the kiss, of how it had made her feel, took the edge off her humiliation. He'd made her want to do something stupid, like run her fingers over that finely muscled chest. To feel him, firm flesh, heat and a hint of chest hair, beneath her palms.

He'd made her want more than that. Her entire body heated at the thought of exactly what he'd made her want.

And he thought it was a mistake. Had he even wanted her? Even a little? Or had he just been horny and wanting sex? And she was in his house instead of one of the women he'd *selected*.

He wouldn't have stopped with one of them. Wouldn't have called it a mistake.

She opened her door and padded down the hall, cracking open the door to Ana's room. She pushed Dante, and the arousal, the need, the hurt he'd inflicted on her, out of her body. A sense of calm washed over her as soon as she entered her daughter's room. She didn't need blood relation, or a government document to feel like Ana was hers. She was, in every sense of the word, no question.

She walked over to the crib and leaned up against the rail, not minding that the wood was digging into her ribs. She bent down and ran her hand over Ana's fuzzy head, down her stomach. Ana sighed and wiggled beneath Paige's hand, making a little smacking sound with her mouth.

So much perfection. So much love. So much responsibility. Paige had never succeeded at anything in her life. And she had to succeed at this.

No matter how hot the kisses, Dante Romani was just a means to an end. She couldn't let him distract her.

And that meant no more kissing. Unless they had to. For the press or for social services.

Suddenly she felt very tired. Like a weight had come to rest on her shoulders. It was harder than she'd imagined it would be. And she couldn't pretend that she didn't care. Couldn't pretend that there wasn't pressure pushing in from all sides. Couldn't pretend that losing would mean nothing.

Not when it would mean everything.

"I'll do my very best, sweetie," she whispered, an ache in her throat, a tear rolling down her face. She just hoped that for once, her best would be good enough.

CHAPTER EIGHT

PAIGE managed to avoid Dante for the next few days. As best as she could avoid someone when she lived with him and drove to work in the same car with him every morning.

She was definitely much more careful when trying to sneak into his room for clothes. Not because she was afraid of him, but because she was afraid of herself.

She'd liked the kiss too much and she was in serious danger of longing after the man. She didn't do the longing thing. It ended in disappointment. And sometimes humiliation. Whether it was test scores or boys, that had been her experience. Longing just made the impossible hurt more.

There was no time for longing. She had to focus on Ana, not her suddenly perky hormones.

She growled into her empty office and bent down, rummaging through the box of glass, glitter-covered ornaments and gathered a few of them in her arms, taking them over to the work space she had cleared for herself in the back of the room.

The sunlight streamed in, bright and perfect for Paige to get an idea of just how everything would glitter in the windows of Colson's department stores at Christmastime. The Christmas designs took up so much of her year, because every year there was the pressure to do bigger, better, more intricate. She loved it.

They moved her wooden frame, the same size and shape

of a standard Colson's window, so that it was right in the path of the sun and she started hanging the ornaments from the top with fishing line.

They caught the light, and they glinted. But it wasn't enough. She needed flash. She needed something no one would walk by and ignore.

She dug through her big box of sparkle, as she'd dubbed it, and produced a canister of silver glitter, one of gold and some deep purple gems. She set to it.

The finished product was much better. They caught fire when the sun hit, and beneath the display lights they would be fantastic.

She brushed her hands on her black skinny jeans and grimaced when she noticed the trail of glitter she'd put down her thighs.

"You've been working hard."

She turned at the sound of Dante's voice and ignored the fact that her heart had slammed into her chest and then started pounding hard and fast.

"Eh, you know the old joke. Hardly working and all that," she said. She wasn't sure why she was so quick to dismiss her work, and yet, she always did. Making light of it seemed to be her default setting. She was only just noticing it, and she didn't like it.

"Doesn't look that way to me," he said, crossing the threshold and moving to her work area. "I like it."

"There will be more. The mannequins, of course. Plus, about fifty more of these hanging at different heights. Snow. A Christmas tree. This is just for one of the side-street windows. But the main window display is going to be pretty amazing. I'm excited."

"I can tell."

"I put a lot of work into it," she said, for herself more than for him. "And I work really hard."

"Of course you do, Paige, or you would hardly still be on my payroll. This will be our third Christmas with you at the helm, and everyone has said how much higher the quality has been on the displays since then."

"Well…thank you."

"Tell me about the main window."

"It's going to be called Visions of Sugarplums. It will be a bunch of Christmas fantasies. And I think I want to have them like they're sort of springing from a dream. So some mist and icicles and lights. Very whimsical and beautiful."

"And all the same at each location?"

"I think each one should be slightly different," she said. "At least the big destination stores in Paris, New York, Berlin, et cetera. So that each one is an attraction."

"Do you have the budget for it?"

"Um, now that you mention it, I do need a slight budget increase."

"I thought you might."

"But you said my displays are high quality."

"I did. How much more do you need?"

She named a sum in the several thousands and Dante didn't bat an eye. "All right, if that's what you need, I will make sure you have it."

"Thank you," she said.

She stopped and really looked at him for the first time since he'd walked in. She'd glanced at him, but she'd avoided careful study. She knew why now. Looking at him full-on was a bit like staring into the sun. He was so beautiful it made her ache. She could no more reach out and touch him, have him for her own, than she could claim a star.

It made her feel so achingly sad. Just for a moment. She didn't have time to worry about Dante or the fact that she had the hots for him. Or the fact that, in all honesty, it felt like more than just having the hots for him.

"Ready for the couples interview?" she asked him.

"Of course," he said, his tone sounding thoroughly unconvincing. Which was funny, because if Dante was one thing, it was certain.

"What are you worried about?"

He looked at her and arched one dark brow. "I don't worry, *cara mia*."

"About anything ever?"

"No."

"What are you doing in business? You should be teaching self-help classes."

He chuckled, a dark sound. "I don't think I'm in much of a position to be telling people how to help themselves. I'm just very good at ignoring things I don't want to deal with."

It was shockingly honest, and it was also something she recognized.

"Yeah, me, too."

"Something we have in common," he said.

"Who would have thought?"

"Not me. Do you think it's enough to play the part of convincing couple?" He took a step closer to her and her stomach quivered. She could taste him on her tongue, the memory of his kiss so strong it was enough to make her knees shake.

Enough to make her take a step toward him. Stupid, really, because she shouldn't kiss him again. He didn't even want to kiss her, she was sure. Because that first time had been a mistake. He'd said so.

He tilted his head to the side, his expression intense, as though he was studying her.

"We certainly have chemistry," he said, his tone rough.

She laughed, shaky, nervous. "You think so?"

He nodded and took another step toward her. "Yes, and it's a good thing, too. Many things can be faked, Paige, and some of them even quite convincingly. But the heat between us? That's real. And no one will question it."

"I don't really know if one kiss constitutes as heat," she said. "One kiss that you said was a mistake."

His lips curved upward. "Are you challenging me?"

"No. I'm not that stupid."

"No, you are certainly not stupid." Strange, but that made

her chest feel warm, made her heart lift. "But you might be trying to bait me into kissing you again."

"Why would I do that?" she asked.

"For the same reason I'm hoping you are baiting me. I'd like to kiss you again."

"You...want to kiss me?"

He nodded.

"B-but last time you said..."

"I said it shouldn't have happened, because we both have goals to focus on. And I think we might both find it hard to focus while we're tangled together in bed. And that, Paige, is where a kiss like the one we shared in my bedroom leads."

"Oh."

"I'm going to kiss you again."

"I don't think that's a great idea."

"Perhaps not, but in just an hour we will be interviewed as a couple, and it's imperative we have no awkwardness between us." He took another step toward her and she could feel his heat, smell the scent of him. Clean skin, soap. Man.

She took a step toward him. His gaze dropped to her mouth and she pulled her lower lip between her teeth.

He reached out and put his thumb on her lip. She raised her focus, her eyes clashing with his. "I find I envy your lip," he said.

He couldn't possibly mean... She touched her tongue to the tip of his thumb, tasting salt, tasting Dante. Then she took a breath and a chance, and bit him gently. He closed his eyes, a rumble of satisfaction vibrating through his chest.

Emboldened, she repeated the action, biting harder this time.

He moved quickly, wrapping both arms around her and pulling her up against his hard body. She pushed up onto her toes and kissed him. It felt so familiar and so foreign at the same time. So wickedly exciting.

He thrust his tongue between her lips and she recipro-cated, the slide and friction sending a shot of heat through her veins. Making her breasts ache to be touched, making her feel hollow.

He put both hands on her hips and gripped her tightly, pulling her against him, letting her feel the hard jut of his arousal against her stomach.

He backed her against the desk and she adjusted so that the edge was just under her butt, supporting her weight. He moved in closer to her, parting her thighs slightly, settling between them.

He pressed his lips to her jaw, her neck, her collarbone.

She never wanted it to stop. She wanted more. And she didn't want to have to look him in the face when it was over and see the same regret she'd seen last night.

The kissing was safe. The kissing was good. She wanted more of that.

But it ended, and when he pulled away, it wasn't horror or regret she saw on his face. It was worse. It was nothing. Nothing but a smooth, beautiful, unreadable mask. Like he hadn't just pushed her to a point she'd never reached before. Like he hadn't introduced her to a whole new side of attraction.

Like the world hadn't just tilted on its axis. Her world certainly had.

"That, I think, proves my point," he said.

She wanted to hit him. Kick him in the shins. Sing a show tune. Something that would get him to react. Because his coolness, his totally unruffled state, was killing her.

"That we have chemistry? Yeah, thanks. I'm really glad I got to be a part of the experiment." She touched her lips. They were hot. And swollen. Overly sensitive just like the rest of her body.

Dante moved slightly and she caught a glimpse of gold shimmer on his suit jacket with the movement.

She frowned. "Could you move to the light here?" She indicated the shaft of sun coming through the window.

He complied, and the order did earn her a strange look,

which, all things considered, she would take and feel somewhat satisfied with.

The light hit his front and a giggle climbed her throat, bursting from her lips. "Oh, my gosh. I'm so sorry!"

"What?"

"Your suit."

He looked down at the spray of golden glitter that was pressed against the entire front of his suit in a little Paige-shaped pattern.

He uttered a curse and brushed his hand over his jacket. Paige tried to hold in her laughter, and succeeded in snorting.

He gave her a dirty look.

"I'm sorry! Oh, brushing it like that isn't going to help. Glitter is the cold sore of the craft world. It spreads easily and it's hard to get rid of."

"Yes," he bit out, "thank you. I actually figured out the reference without it being explained."

"You were the one who pulled me all up against you. I was working, as we established, and that involves…"

"It's fine, Paige," he said, his annoyance, probably with the whole situation, coming through now.

"I am sorry. Because that suit must have cost…"

"A lot," he ground out, "but I have a lot so it's not a big deal."

Except that he was meticulous with his things to a degree she couldn't wrap her mind around, so she knew on some level it was a big deal.

"Well, then…"

"I have some things to finish up and then I'll meet you at the day care to pick Ana up."

Dante had been forced to walk through the office advertising intimate contact with his own personal glitter fairy. Which, he imagined, he should be somewhat grateful for or at the very least, okay with.

She was, after all, supposed to be his fiancée, and that

meant they were expected to touch. To kiss. To have interludes in her office during the workday.

He should be fine with it, but he wasn't, and it had nothing to do with the possible ruination of his suit and everything to do with the flashing sign on his chest that was advertising his loss of control.

There were only a few minutes left until their interview. He stepped out of a cold shower and into his bedroom. He dressed quickly, ignoring the ache in his body that reminded him that no amount of icy-cold shower could steal the desire he had for her.

He gritted his teeth and turned sharply, hitting the solid wood bedpost with his open palm. The pain, he hoped, would remind him to keep himself under control. A reminder that passion had its price. That any loss of control had a cost.

Nothing was free. Nothing was without consequence.

The sting in his palm reminded him, for a moment, of her teeth grazing over his thumb. Of the reaction that faint pain had had on his body.

He closed his eyes and hit the bedpost again, the hard wood pushing past flesh and making contact with the bone in his wrist. He lowered his hand and shook it.

There was a timid knock on his door. "Come in."

"Oh, hi. I was wondering if you were ready?" Paige opened the door wide to reveal her and Ana. They were both dressed in pink. Paige in a bright, silk dress and Ana in pale pink one, her chubby legs swinging back and forth.

"I am now," he said, running his stinging hand over his hair.

"Good, she's almost here." Paige turned and flitted out of the room and he followed her. Paige had adjusted Ana so that she was up against her chest, Ana's bright eyes peeking over Paige's shoulder. Looking right at him.

He had no experience with babies, and no particular desire to become experienced with them. And this one, this tiny, perfectly formed human, seemed to look straight into him. As if she could see everything. And yet, her expression remained clear and bright. As if she saw it all, and it made no difference.

He realized then that there was one thing that had been neglected. He and Paige were meant to present themselves as a couple, but he'd forgotten that Ana would be with them. That he would have to find some ease with her, as well.

Suddenly, Ana's little face crumpled and she let out a high-pitched whine. Paige stopped completely, adjusting the baby's position, stroking her little cheek. It was amazing to see the effect Ana had on Paige. The little whirlwind of a woman was serene with her daughter in her arms. Her focus entirely on her.

Ana squeaked again and Paige started to sing. A soft, sweet sound. A lullaby. Terror curled around his heart, terror he hadn't anticipated, and couldn't shake off.

Paige bent forward, her necklace falling toward Ana as she continued to sing.

Cold sweat broke out over his skin, a sick, heavy weight hitting him in the gut and just lying there in him.

He knew one lullaby. And it was in Italian. If he closed his eyes, he could see his mother, leaning over his bed, her necklace hanging down, just as Paige's was doing now. Singing softly, her hand comforting on his forehead.

Stella, stellina,
la notte si avvicina
Star, little star, the night is approaching…

He shook off the memory, but it tried to hold him, tried to make him see it all. His mother, first alive and so beautiful, and then…

He swallowed hard and took in a breath. "Let's go," he said, his voice too rough, too harsh.

Paige's head snapped up and she looked at him with startled eyes. It made his heart twist. "Sorry," she said.

He shook his head. "No, I'm sorry. I am not myself today."

He wished that were true. Sadly, he feared he was more himself today than he ever usually allowed himself to be.

"Well, get it together. If you blow this...if we blow this... I can't lose her."

He looked at the little, fussing baby, and back at the woman who was, in every way that mattered, her mother.

"I know," he said, teeth gritted, heart pounding.

They couldn't blow it. Paige couldn't lose Ana, he knew that. But more importantly, Ana couldn't lose her. Because he knew, better than most, just how much of a loss it would be.

"Did it go well? I think it went well." Paige knew she was chattering, but she couldn't help herself.

The interview was over and they were out on the terrace on the second floor of the house. Dante's housekeeper had barbecued for them, and they were sitting now, their plates empty, looking out at the ocean. Ana was lying happily on her stomach on a large cushion that had been placed out for her, rocking back and forth and flailing her hands and feet.

"I think it went fine," Dante said.

There was no sign of the dark, angry man who had been in the hall earlier. There hadn't been any sign of him from the moment Rebecca Addler had walked through the door.

He'd charmed her, utterly. Clearly, the media's stories about him hadn't bothered her in the least or, if they had, Dante in the flesh had erased them in a moment.

He had that effect, that ability to make everything seem fine and easy. He exuded total and complete confidence, no matter the situation. He certainly interviewed better than she did, which was galling, because it showed her just how faulty something like this could be. She was the one who loved Ana, with all of her heart, and yet, he was the one who had charmed the social worker.

Thank God he was on her team.

"Well, I'm glad you're feeling confident."

"Why worry, Paige, the outcome will be the same either way."

"Easy for you to say. She's...everything to me."

"I know," he said, his tone serious. "And, I swear I will not let you lose her. Whatever it takes."

"Really? Why? Why would you...why would you do that?"

"Because I know what it is to lose a mother," he said, his tone cold. "I know what it is to drift from home to home, no one wanting you. That she is being spared the brunt of it, because of you... I will always have her be spared from it, and if I can help in any way then I will."

She looked over at Ana, and for the first time, she let the fear that was always ready to pounce on her, overtake her fully. "Can I do this? Am I really the best person?" She looked at Dante. "Tell me. Because I'm scared I'm going to mess it up."

He looked stunned for a moment. "I...I confess, I'm not the best person to judge how healthy a family is. But you love her. I remember love. I remember when I could feel it. I remember my mother. And the way you hold her, the way she feels when you're near, that's what it is."

A lump in her throat tried to block her words. "But I mess everything up," she said. "Ask anyone. My family, my teachers, my friends. I always got such bad grades in school. In math and science and history. I liked to read. I did well in English and art. But the other stuff...I could hardly pass a class. I did so poorly that my parents wouldn't help me get to college. And of course I couldn't get a scholarship. And no one was surprised. Because they just...expect it from me." She blinked back tears. "I have messed up about every major life moment a person has. First kisses, prom, getting into college. What if I screw this up, too?"

"You haven't messed everything in your life up," he said, taking on that confident tone that was so familiar to her now. "You do well at your job. Exceedingly well. You lost your best friend and you carried on, both with work and with raising her child. Do you know how many people would have been content to simply let the State take over? So many, Paige. And you didn't do that. You come through when it matters."

"But I'm scared to want it," she said. "I'm scared of how much I care for her."

He frowned and looked out at the sea, the lines by his eyes deepening. "Emotion is the single most dangerous thing I can think of. The kind that controls you. Makes you do things you never thought you were capable of. But...I can see the way it pushes you with her. You told the social worker you were engaged to your boss. You were willing to do anything, take any risk, for her. There is power in that. And your love seems to have power for good. Trust that."

His words were encouraging in a way, but so laced with a bitter sadness that they settled in her like lead.

"And what about your emotions?" she asked. "What power do you see in them?"

He looked at her, his dark eyes glittering. "I looked in myself, and saw the potential for terrible things. And since that day I haven't felt anything. I find my power from somewhere else, a place I can control."

She felt like someone had reached into her chest, grabbed her heart and squeezed it tight. "Dante...you're helping me. I look in you and I see so much good."

"Then you are blind." He stood up and walked off the terrace into the house, and all she could do was stare at his back retreating into the shadows.

She'd seen that emptiness again. That same look he'd gotten in the hall just before he'd snapped at her. That same look he'd had in her office when they'd kissed. She'd taken it for emotionlessness but it wasn't that.

It was something else. Something worse. Something she was afraid she couldn't help him with.

CHAPTER NINE

HE heard crying. He moved to a sitting position in bed and swung his legs over the side, his feet planted on the carpet.

Ana was crying.

He stood and walked out of his room, striding down the hall. He opened the door to the nursery, casting a sliver of light into the room. He saw Paige, sitting in the rocking chair, holding Ana, rocking her, patting her back. Ana was crying still. And so was Paige. Glittery tracks down her cheeks.

His first instinct was to turn away. To walk away from the scene as quickly as possible, go back to bed. Shut down the strange emotions that were rising up, pressing on his throat.

"Is everything okay?"

"No," Paige said thickly. "She's been crying for an hour and she won't stop. I've tried everything. I fed her, I changed her. I'm holding her. I turned the light on, I turned it off. I don't know what else to do."

"I'm sure it's nothing you're doing wrong."

"What if it is?" she whispered, despair lacing her voice.

He took a step into the room, ignoring the tightness in his chest. "Babies cry, for no reason sometimes."

He'd heard that said, though he wasn't sure where.

"But Ana doesn't, usually."

"Does she have a fever?" That seemed a logical question.

Paige put her cheek down on Ana's head. "I don't think

so." She smoothed her hands over the baby's brow. "She doesn't feel warm to me. Does she feel warm to you?"

He couldn't bring himself to touch her. She was a tiny creature, fragile. Small-boned. Delicate. He didn't want to put his hands on her.

"I don't think she's warm," he said.

Paige put her hand on the baby's forehead. "No, you're right. I don't think she is. Could you sing to her?"

"Sing?" he asked.

"A lullaby."

His breath stalled in his throat, got trapped there. "I don't know any lullabies," he lied.

"Oh...that's okay." She patted Ana on the back. "I tried to sing and she just cried harder so I thought maybe you could..."

"Sorry," he said, curling his fingers into fists, fighting the urge to run from the room.

For that reason alone he had to stay. Dante Romani did not run. He would not.

Ana hiccuped, her tiny shoulders jerking with the motion. Her cries slowed, quieted, until they became muffled, sporadic whimpers.

He watched her for a few moments, silence settling between them as Paige continued to rock Ana until the whimpering ceased altogether.

"See, she was just crying," he said, trying to sound certain. Trying to feel some control over the situation when the simple fact was, he had none. There was a nursery in his home. There was a baby here. A woman. She had her things in his closet.

No, nothing was in his control anymore.

"I guess she was," Paige whispered.

She got up from the chair and walked over to the crib, placing Ana gingerly onto the mattress, then straightening, freezing for a second while she waited to see if the baby would wake up.

The room stayed silent.

"She seems like she's asleep now," Paige whispered.

"You should sleep, too," he said. She looked tired. Sad.

She wrapped her robe around herself, a little tremor shaking her body. "No. I don't…I don't think I could sleep right now."

The desolation in her tone did something to him. Made his stomach feel tight.

"Hungry?" he asked.

She shook her head. "Not really. But do you have chocolate?"

He let out a long, slow breath. Paige was upset, obviously, and while he would usually walk away and get back in bed without a twinge of guilt, he couldn't do that now. He wasn't going to take the time to analyze why. "We'll have to go raid the cupboards and find out. I'm not certain."

"How can you not be sure if you have chocolate?" They walked out of the nursery and left the door open so they could hear Ana if she woke.

"I'm not accustomed to raiding my kitchen at odd hours."

"I guess that's why you have washboard abs and I don't." Her eyes were trained meaningfully on his bare torso. Her complete lack of guile amused him, and aroused him. She didn't try to hide her open appraisal of him. And yet, it was different than the sort of open gazes he was used to seeing. There was no extra motive with Paige, only admiration.

He looked back at her, treating her to the same, intense study she'd treated him to. Her T-shirt molded to her breasts, her pajama pants sitting low on her hips. Too baggy for his taste. He wanted to see the curves beneath. "I have no complaints about your figure."

She stopped and turned sharply. "Oh, really?"

He shouldn't have said that. There was no point in fostering the attraction between Paige and himself. It wasn't good for either of them. She did something to him. Tested him in ways he'd never been tested before.

Detachment was normally simple for him. This time, not

so much. But he couldn't pull the compliment back now. He wasn't the sort of man to lie to a woman, or charm her to get her into bed, but he still knew enough to know that this was a subject to tread carefully with. Could sense that the wrong words could break her, or lead her to believe he could give things he simply could not.

"Every inch of you is beautiful," he said. It was the truth, not flattery. Though why he was compelled to speak it in that way, he wasn't certain.

She flushed scarlet. "You haven't seen every inch of me."

"Yet," he said, the word escaping without his permission and hanging between them, heavy and, he realized in that moment, stating the inevitable.

"No," she said, turning away from him and continuing down the stairs and into the kitchen.

"No?"

"You and I both know it would be a very bad idea."

"Why is that, Paige?" he asked. "What harm could come from a bit of fun?" There was so much wrong with that sentence. He knew exactly what harm resulted from sex and passion. Which was precisely why his sexual encounters were void of passion. Passion wasn't required for release. It was perfunctory. The right contact in the right place and his partners found their pleasure, then he was free to take his. Find a moment of blinding oblivion. But it had very little to do with the woman he was with, and even less to do with feeling.

And *fun* was a word he wasn't sure he put any stock in. He wasn't sure if he ever had any.

"Quite a few bits of harm, I think," she said, crossing to the stainless-steel refrigerator and opening the freezer, rummaging through the contents. "What ho! Chocolate ice cream!"

She pulled the carton out and held it high like a frozen trophy before setting in on the granite countertop. "Get spoons," she said. "And bowls."

"And the previous discussion is closed?"

"Yep."

He complied with her order and produced bowls and spoons. He set them out and scooped them both some ice cream. He pulled up on the edge of the counter and sat, and Paige did the same on the counter across from him.

"Maybe I won't be such a terrible mother," she said, eating a spoonful of ice cream.

"You won't be. But what has led you to the conclusion?"

"I used my stern voice and got you to change the subject and dish my ice cream," she said, her grin impish. But the impishness didn't reach her eyes. She still looked sad. Scared.

"I want to tell you something," he said. He lied. He didn't want to tell her what he was about to say, but it seemed important. It was all he had to offer.

She nodded and took another bite of ice cream, her eyes trained on his.

"Do you know what I remember about my mother?" he asked.

She blinked hard, her eyes glistening. She set her bowl and spoon down on the counter beside her. "No."

"I was six when she died. But I do remember her. How good it felt when she put her hand on my forehead before I fell asleep. The way her voice sounded, soothing, kind. The way she sang to me." He cleared his throat. "It's not about getting everything right. It's about those things, those small things. That's all that matters. You do that for Ana. You may make mistakes, but you'll be the constant, comforting presence in her life. That's what matters," he repeated.

He remembered more about his mother. Her fear. When his father would come home from work in a dark mood. Her tucking him in, locking his door with a key. So he couldn't get out and see. So his father couldn't get in and cause him any harm.

And he remembered her lying on the floor, too still. Too pale. The sparkle gone from her eyes forever.

He remembered lying with her on the floor and singing her

a lullaby until the police came. His hand on her head, stroking her hair, like she had always done for him.

Stella, Stellina. Star, little star.

He left that part out. If only he could leave it out of his mind. If only he could scrub the memory away. Hold on to the good, leave out the bad. But it wasn't possible.

The good always came with bad. Always.

A tear slipped down Paige's cheek. "She must have been wonderful."

"She was," he said.

"I have failed at so many things," she said. "And I don't know why. I don't know why things are harder for me. I tried to do well in school...I just couldn't. And my parents...I think they tried to be supportive of me, but I don't think they really believed that I was trying. My brother and sister, they were extraordinary, and they worked for it. But I had to work for ordinary. I had to bust my butt just to be average. And that meant no college for me. In their minds...I suppose I was a failure. I mean, I had my art but art doesn't translate to much, not to them."

"And that's why you moved."

She nodded. "To find out what it would be like if I wasn't surrounded by people who expected nothing from me. People who had given up on me. Shyla always believed in me. She said I was smart. No one ever said that. No one else. She encouraged me to go out for the position at Colson's and I thought...I thought there was no way. I had no degree, no experience. But your hiring manager...she saw something in me, too. In my work. She took a chance on me, and the only reason I was brave enough to take a chance on myself was because of my friend. I can't let her down," she said, her voice shaky. "There is so much at stake here and I can't fail. But failure is something I'm so good at, I'm afraid history will just repeat itself."

"Tell me, are your bother and sister artists?"

She shook her head. "No."

"Your parents, are they artists?"

"No."

"Could any of them imagine the window settings that you do? Not only that, could they find the materials, imagine the lighting, the colors, everything that you do, to make them a reality?"

"Probably not."

"Then maybe you haven't failed. You've simply succeeded in different areas. Areas that those other people couldn't, and so don't understand."

"I…" She blinked rapidly. "You're the first person who's ever…said it like that."

"It's true, though. We can't all be great at everything. I couldn't design the windows for the store, so I hired you to do it."

"Your hiring manager did."

"Fine, but you get the idea. I don't do everything. I don't have the ability to do everything. Why should you?"

"It's just that what I do has never been important to my family."

"That's their problem. You're good at what counts. You stand firm when you're needed. You're coming through for Ana. Your instinct, when you were being interviewed by the social worker, was to protect her, to keep her with you no matter what. If that doesn't prove that you're strong enough to do this, nothing will."

She slid down from the counter, her hands balled into fists at her sides. She took a sharp breath and crossed to him, standing in front of him, eye level to his chest. She reached up and put her hands on his cheeks, then tugged his face down as she drew up onto her tiptoes, pressing her lips against his.

He held on to the edge of the counter, letting her lead the kiss, letting her part his lips with her tongue. Letting her set the pace, the intensity.

He could taste the salt from her tears on her mouth, could feel the barely contained sadness in each shaking breath.

He ached to take control. To tug her up against him and to kiss her with every bit of pent-up passion, sorrow and pain that was buried inside of him. That was threatening to claw its way out through his chest if he didn't find a way to release it.

But he couldn't allow it.

This was for her, to have what she would. He would give it to her, and feel no sense of sacrifice. Whatever she wanted, she could have. As long as the true control belonged to him.

Paige pulled back from Dante, her heart thundering, her hands shaking. She didn't know what she was thinking, if she was thinking. All she knew was that she wanted to feel something big. Something real and affirming. She wanted Dante's actions to confirm his words.

She wanted to prove that she could want someone, and have them want her. That she wasn't broken. That she wasn't a joke. She wanted the unobtainable, beautiful man all for herself.

She didn't want happily ever after from him. She didn't want love. And she didn't want to thank him. It was something else, a need so deep and raw that she could hardly understand it.

All she knew was that his touch would make things better. His kiss would heal so many wounds, be the confirmation for what he'd spoken.

To prove that she wasn't a failure with men. That she wasn't undesirable. That someone could want her.

She smoothed her hands over his chest, his muscles hot and hard beneath her palms, his chest hair crisp. So sexy and masculine. So different from her own body.

"I want you," she said, her lips still pressed against his.

The silence that followed seemed to last forever. He might reject her. He probably would. But this was the first time she'd ever been willing to take the chance. It felt like a chain had been loosened on her, like she could move more freely.

He slid down from the counter, locking his arm around

her waist and drawing her hard up against his body. "You want to kiss me? Or you want more?"

"M-more."

"I have to hear you say it," he said, his tone stretched, tortured.

"I want to…to sleep with you tonight." A sudden, horrifying thought occurred to her, and her stomach sank to her toes. "Unless you don't want to." Why would he? He'd pulled away from every kiss they'd shared. He was a bronzed god of a man with a physique that looked too good to be real. A man with tons of sexual experience. A man who could have, and had had, any woman he wished. For a crazy moment she'd been convinced she could have this, could have him. But maybe she'd been fooling herself. Again.

He chuckled, rough and humorless. "How can you think I don't want you?"

"I'm average, remember?"

He moved his hand up to her hair and pushed his fingers through it, tugging on a pink strand, rubbing it between his thumb and forefinger. "I have never seen anyone quite like you. Which means the description cannot be accurate."

"You hate my hair."

He shook his head. "It's growing on me."

He pressed his other hand against her lower back and brought her into closer contact with his body. With the evidence of his desire for her.

Her eyes widened. "You do want me."

"I'm sorry it's so hard for you to believe. But by the end of tonight, it won't be."

She wished she had a witty reply, something to defuse the tension. Something to loosen the knot in her stomach and lessen the ache between her thighs. To lessen the importance of the moment. But there was nothing. Her brain was too busy spinning around all the ways he could show her.

Never before had discovering what she'd been missing with sex been so important. Been so essential. But it was now.

He kissed her again, intensifying it. He moved his hand down to the waistband of her pajama pants and let his finger-tips drift beneath the flannel fabric, and down low so that he was palming her butt, his touch hot and rough and perfect. He squeezed her and a shot of liquid, sexual heat poured through her, zipping straight to her core.

She arched into him, rubbing her breasts against his chest, looking for a way to dull the ache there, squirming as the one between her thighs intensified, the hand on her bottom so close to where she needed him, the nearness making it all the more frustrating.

"We have to find a bed," she said, pulling away from him, her breath coming in out-of-control gasps.

"We don't need a bed," he growled, leaning in, kissing her neck.

"Oh. *Oh...*" Her mind went blank for a moment as his tongue swirled over the hollow in her throat. "Yes. We do. I don't feel like...I don't have the experience to..." She was not going to say virgin. She was going to avoid that word at all costs. "I'm remedial. At this. I need something standard. And soft. In case I fall or something."

He stopped for a moment, his dark eyes searching hers. "I won't let you fall."

You might not be able to stop me. The words hovered on the edge of her lips, but she didn't speak them. She didn't dare. She wasn't even sure what they meant. Only that they terrified her down to her bones.

"I know but...please?"

He nodded and swung her up into his arms. She squeaked and clung to his neck as he walked out of the kitchen and to the stairs, taking them two at a time. He didn't put her down until they were in his room, at the foot of his bed.

"Will this bed do?"

She nodded, her throat dry. "Yes. Now come here and kiss me. I promise not to get glitter on you."

He moved to her, cupping her cheek and brushing his thumb across her skin. "Your wish is my command."

He kissed her, deeply, sensually, his hands roaming over her curves. He cupped her breast, teasing her nipple with light contact, making her ache for more. For his flesh on hers. His mouth on her body.

He tugged her shirt up over her head. The cold air hit her breasts, and she didn't have any time to feel self-conscious about what he was seeing. He tugged her against him and she gasped as her breasts brushed against his chest, the heat of his skin warming her through her whole body, his chest hair abrading her sensitized nipples.

She moved her hands over his back, his muscles shifting and bunching beneath her fingertips.

He pushed her flannel pajamas and underwear down her hips, letting them pool at her feet. She was thankful he hadn't paused to look at her panties. A sexual interlude had been the last thing on her mind when she'd selected the purple cotton garment after her shower that evening.

She wanted to take his clothes off him, but her hands felt heavy suddenly, clumsy. She wasn't sure if it was her move or not. Or if he liked it when a woman undressed him. Or… anything.

He was so perfect, so beautiful, just like the moment. She didn't want to do anything to mess it up.

Thankfully, he was more than ready and willing to discard his own clothes, and after he disappeared into the bathroom briefly, he returned, fully erect, more gorgeous than any man had a right to be, and carrying a box of condoms.

She couldn't stop staring at him. At the thick erection that stood out from his body. She'd never seen a naked man in person before, and pictures of classical statues really didn't do them justice. Or at least, they didn't represent Dante.

"I want to touch you," she said, shocked at her boldness. But for some reason, the moment he'd come back into the bedroom, all of her nerves had evaporated. She was standing there, naked, and he was there, naked. And they were about to share the most intimate connection two people could possibly share.

There was no room for fear. Or shame, or awkwardness. She was sure. It was such an unusual feeling for her. And yet, with him, in the moment, everything felt right.

"Feel free," he said, his voice rough.

She moved to him, ran her fingers from his chest down to his abs, to the dark line of hair that led from there and to his hard, thick shaft. She wrapped her fingers around him, testing his weight.

"What do you like?" she asked, her heart thundering hard, her stomach quivering.

"This," he said, his breath hissing through his teeth.

"Just me touching you?"

"Yes," he said. His breathing increased, his chest rising and falling quickly.

"And this?" She squeezed him gently and was rewarded with a groan that bordered on tortured.

"Yes," he bit out.

"Harder?"

He put his hand over hers and stilled her movements. "Only if you want me to come right now."

She pulled her hand back. "No. Not yet. You aren't allowed yet."

"I thought not." He captured her lips in a fierce kiss, bringing her down onto the bed with him.

She looped her thigh over his hip, opening herself to him. She moved against him, each brush of his arousal against the bundle of nerves at the apex of her thighs sending a streak of white heat through her.

He lowered his head and sucked her nipple deep into his mouth. A raw moan escaped her lips and she gripped his shoulders hard, her nails digging into his skin. He lifted his head, letting it fall back. She gripped him harder and he winced, his hold tightening on her back.

"Don't stop," she said.

And he obeyed, lowering his head to her breasts again, licking her, sucking her, bringing her to the edge and back with the sensual assault from his mouth. He moved his hand from her back, down to her waist, to her hips, holding her hard, kissing a path down her body until he came to the place that was wet and aching for him.

His tongue moved over her clitoris and she lifted her hips off the bed, sensation so deep, so intense hitting her that she couldn't hold still. He held her, continuing as though she wasn't whimpering beneath him, as though her body wasn't trembling, her world crumbling inward, reducing to pleasure, to Dante.

She laced her fingers into his hair, holding him to her, so close now, so close to the peak that she had no desire to fight it. No desire to fight him.

He released his hold on her and his hand joined his mouth, one finger sliding deep inside of her as he flicked his tongue over her clitoris again. The world exploded behind her eyelids. Stars raining down on her, leaving her blanketed in heat and light.

She shook, her body trembling as each wave of release passed through her.

Dante lifted his head and kissed her hip, the space just beneath her belly button. Her stomach. Between her breasts. Then he settled between her thighs, his hardness probing the soft, wet entrance to her body.

He cursed and paused, reaching beside them and picking up the condom box. He fished inside of it for a moment, producing a small packet that he tore open quickly. He rolled the condom onto his length with deft efficiency, and she was grateful he hadn't asked her to do it.

Then he was back over her, pressing into her. She felt a brief, searing pain as he pushed inside of her, her body stretching to accommodate him.

He paused for a moment, his dark eyes blazing, his expression pained.

She shook her head. And he didn't speak. Instead, he thrust into her to the hilt, his body coming up hard against hers, making contact right where she needed it, pleasure erasing the pain, slowly, but oh so perfectly.

He retreated, thrusting home again, establishing a steady rhythm that built up tension inside of her again. It was deeper this time, reaching farther inside of her, calling up the need from somewhere new. It was shared desperation, shared need.

She met each thrust, working with him, moving with him, toward completion. Everything blurred, blending together, the room beyond Dante turning fuzzy, insubstantial.

His movements became erratic, evidence of his fraying control, and hers began to shred, too. Her grip on the world loosening. When they fell, they fell together, raw sounds of completion filling the room as they reached the peak.

She held on to him tightly, trying to keep from getting lost in it all. Anchoring him to her.

When his muscles stopped trembling, he let out a long, slow breath and pressed his forehead against her chest. She wrapped her arms around him and held him there. Held his body against hers, skin to skin, every inch of him against every inch of her.

She didn't want to speak. She didn't want to move. She didn't want to face reality.

But she knew that they would have to.

But not yet.

CHAPTER TEN

DANTE cursed himself. To hell. To any level of hell. He'd heard every reference about his name in connection with the place of suffering and damnation that the media could possibly create, and this time, he found it appropriate.

He belonged there for this.

He had let her lead, but what he hadn't realized was that she hadn't known the dance.

A virgin. A damn virgin.

He should have known. He should have seen it in every wide-eyed glance, in every sweet, perfect blush. In the way she didn't seem to know the sort of power her body could wield.

But he hadn't, or worse, he'd ignored it. That black part of his soul rising up to choke out the control, choke out the small seed of human decency that had still rested inside of him.

He avoided women who didn't know the game. Who didn't understand that with him sex was only about one thing: release. Even if the woman had had a hundred partners, he had to be sure she understood that.

But a woman who had no experience with sex? She was not the kind of player he picked for the game. Ever.

The voice in his head whispering that Paige was different was silenced completely.

"Dammit, Paige," he said, his voice rough.

"Oh, no. Don't do that please."

She scooted away from him and burrowed under his covers. In his bed. Like she was planning on staying the night, which he was sure she was. Women didn't stay the night with him. They never had. Not once.

They met in hotels. They got the itch scratched. They left. A long encounter lasted a couple of hours. Never more.

"Don't get upset about you not telling me you were a virgin?" he growled.

"Yes!" She threw her arms up and brought her hands back down on the covers. "It's stupid. You're not a mustache-twirling villain who just ripped away my maidenhead. I knew what I was doing."

He moved into a sitting position on the edge of the bed and forked his fingers through his hair, his heart pounding heavily. Too quickly. He hadn't gotten his control back yet. "I cannot even wrap my head around that sentence."

"I *wanted* it. I told you I wanted it. You asked me to say it, and I did. I wanted to sleep with you. I wanted you to be my first. No, you know, that's not even it. It wasn't about first. It was about wanting you. End of story."

"Paige, I don't... I can't offer you anything."

"Oh, you mean you can't offer me anything other than a temporary marriage to help me keep custody of my daughter? You can't offer me anything more than that and multiple orgasms? Is that what you mean?"

"Paige," he growled.

"Get into bed, Dante."

"I don't..." He was about to tell her. To tell her that his lovers did not share his bed. His lovers didn't usually enter his home.

But the words stuck in his throat. He should tell her, tell her that if she wanted sex, she could have it, but if she wanted to make love she would have to look somewhere else. But for the first time in his memory, the blunt words, the true words, stuck in his throat.

He stood. "I need to go and take care of things."

She nodded, her hands clutching the covers like talons, as if proving to him that she was well and truly rooted to the spot.

He walked into the bathroom and disposed of the condom, then for the second time in only a few days, he gripped the edge of the sink and regarded the man in the mirror.

He released his hold and straightened, turning away from his reflection. And he weighed which sin would be greater. To give her what she asked for, with no intention, no ability, to offer emotion. Or to show her now, that with him, there would be no softness.

He walked back into the bedroom, his chest tightening when he saw Paige, deep in the blankets, rolled onto her side, her eyes open.

"You did come back," she said.

"I did," he said.

His stomach tightened, painfully, a raw, intense tremor of terror working its way beneath his skin and straight into his heart. The closer he got to the bed, the sharper the feeling became.

He stopped, trying to catch his breath. She looked…angelic. Her lips swollen and flushed pink, her skin still flushed, too. Her blue eyes filled with an innocent expectancy, a need that he knew he could never meet.

And still, the desire to slide beneath the sheets and tug her bare body against his was strong. The need to feast on her beauty, to sate himself on that need, so great, so powerful, it threatened to take over.

He took a step backward. "You are welcome to stay in here for the night, Paige," he said, his words stilted. "But I have work to do."

He bent and retrieved his pants from the floor, tugged them on, then did the same with his shirt. And without looking back, he walked out of the room and closed the door firmly behind him.

* * *

Paige opened her eyes slowly, squinting against the light coming through the curtains. Her first thought was that it was strange that Ana hadn't woken up.

Her next thought was about how strange it was that she was naked. She never slept naked. She wore her pajamas. But she hadn't last night.

Oh, yes, and now she remembered, very, very clearly why she hadn't worn pajamas.

Dante. His hands. His mouth. His body. He was...everything a man should be. No wonder she'd been so fascinated with him for so long. Somehow, some part of her, must have known, instinctively, that that man was capable of giving pleasure that went well beyond anything she'd previously imagined.

A smile curved her lips. Okay, so she hadn't waited for marriage, or even true love, which she was sure her perfect sister had done. But it had been worth it. So, so worth it.

She pushed away the dreaded suspicion that she might feel differently about it later, and instead, focused on the warm satisfaction that was still resting in her body. She shifted and winced. Oh, yeah, there was also a little bit of *ow* resting in her body, but that seemed worth it, too.

Her muscles hurt. And so did...things that had never hurt before.

She rolled over and realized that the sheets were cold where Dante should have been. And then she remembered him walking out, his expression shuttered, blank, and she wondered if he had ever come back to bed.

The door to the bedroom swung open and Dante entered, wearing the clothes from the night before.

"Good morning," she said, feeling slightly less blissful than she had a second earlier.

He frowned. "It is morning." He tugged his shirt up over his head and her brain stalled at watching the play of perfect, golden skin over shifting muscles.

A little thrill assaulted her. He was hot, so supposedly

out of her league, and yet, last night, he'd been hers. He had wanted her. Her.

She'd gotten the hot guy, and for a moment, she just wanted to celebrate that. Before reality hit.

"Yes, it is morning," she said, sounding far chirpier than she imagined he might like.

"Are you okay?"

She sat up, holding the covers to her chest, and poked herself in the arm. "I…feel okay."

"Very funny, Paige. You know what I'm asking." He dropped his pants and her stomach followed the trajectory, sinking around her toes.

"If I'm angry that you made love with me and left me for the rest of the night?" she asked, keeping her eyes trained on his tight butt as he looked through his closet, shoving her clothing aside with rough, frustrated movements. "I'm a little angry about that, yeah."

"That isn't what I was asking."

She really hoped that he wasn't actually asking what she thought he might be asking, because that was just too stupid. "You want to know if I regret the sex."

"Yes."

She let out an exasperated breath. "I don't regret the sex, Dante. But I am a little put out by the way you acted after. And actually, the way you're acting now."

"It sounds to me like you regret anything happened at all."

"I told you I wanted it," she said, exasperation lacing her tone.

He draped a pair of black slacks and a white shirt over his arm, still completely naked. "I know, but that was before you knew…"

"Just because I was a virgin doesn't mean I didn't know anything about sex. You can know about things without actually doing them."

"But you don't know how they'll make you feel."

"I feel—felt, because now I'm a little annoyed—satisfied. And warm. And…happy until you ditched me to work or whatever it was you did."

"So, you have it all figured out then, do you?"

"Yes. If you stop treating me like a child, or a stranger who invaded your bedroom, I think we can work something out."

His expression turned dark, fierce. He stalked over to the bed and leaned in, planting his hands on the foot of it. "So you think we can just go on and have an affair while you're living here? Just sex. You, me, this bed, no clothes, no emotions—is that what you think?"

He was challenging her, trying to make her back off, trying to make her say no. And she knew it wasn't for her benefit, not really. She didn't know how she knew, but she did.

"Yeah," she said, shrugging one bare shoulder, "I think we could do that."

He raised both eyebrows. "You do?"

"Yeah. Last night was…really fun."

"Fun?" he asked, his tone deadly.

"I can't believe I waited so long. Well, I can, because you know…this is really embarrassing, but when I was in high school, I made out with this guy, but I had braces, and he cut his tongue."

Dante blinked. "He…cut his tongue?"

"Yeah, on the braces. Only because he kissed like an overzealous puppy. You're much better, by the way."

"Thank you," he said, drily.

"You're welcome. Anyway, that's hard to live down." She drew her knees up beneath the covers and studied the stitching on the comforter. "And so, already I was sort of a running joke at the school. And then…senior prom, this guy who was…waaaay out of my league, asked if I would be his date. And I said yes. And then after the dance part, he told me he had a blanket and some drinks waiting for us under the bleachers which means…well, you know what that means. Well, no guy had paid attention to me in a couple of years thanks to the braces incident and so I…I was going to do it."

"But clearly you didn't," he said, straightening.

"Clearly," she said. "Because that wasn't really what I was there for."

"What happened?" he asked.

She bit her lip. "I don't know why it's so hard to talk about. It's been what…four years? Stupid." She shook her head, trying to stop the burning sting of tears in her eyes, the echoing burn of shame in her chest. "We went out to the football field, under the, um…bleachers. It was prom, you know, so…you know."

"Yes," he said, his tone hard. "I know."

"Anyway things were going well. We were kissing, I hadn't injured him. He started to take my dress off…." She blinked hard, trying to keep her tears from falling. She'd cried enough about it. "Then he grabbed my arm and pulled me out onto the football field, and the big lights came on, and a huge group of my *friends* in the senior class threw eggs at me. Laughed at me. They took pictures of me, half-naked like that and trying to cover myself up. They made fliers later to pass out in school."

She bit her lip hard. "You know, I would have gotten in serious trouble, for being out there unauthorized, but I think the principal thought I'd suffered enough. My parents thought so, too. Because everyone saw it. Everyone knew. I don't know why…I don't know why I walked into that. As one of the girls put it, did you really think he came out here to be with *you*?" A tear slid down her cheek and she brushed it away. "I had. I had really believed it. But not after that. And they never let it go. They brought it up all the time, even after graduation, and they would just…laugh like it had been the funniest, cleverest prank of all time. And I learned to laugh, too. Because my only other option was showing how much it hurt and I wouldn't…I didn't want to do that."

"But then you moved here. Away from those people surely…"

"And take a chance at being rejected again? Obviously not

on a scale that grand, but still. My entire senior class made a joke out of my half-naked body."

Dante swore harshly. "There's nothing wrong with your body."

"Maybe not. No...I mean I know there isn't but...they said there was. And in high school that's all that matters."

"Paige, why did you sleep with me?" he asked.

She looked up at him. "You wanted me."

She could see the horror that passed through his eyes clearly. "Is that all? Because you thought I was the only man who would want you? Those people you went to school with were stupid. As limited as your family when it comes to see-ing beauty and value," he bit out. "I cannot imagine any man not wanting you. So I sincerely hope that this wasn't some desperate act of someone who believed they could never have anyone else."

She shook her head. "No. No, that wasn't it. It was... you wanted me, yes, and I could see it. But also...I wanted you. Enough to risk the rejection. I've never wanted anyone enough to put myself out there again. But I wanted you that much. And that seems like a good enough reason to have sex to me."

"And now...now that you've seen that I'm not a support-ive, caring lover. Do you regret it?"

Yes, his abandonment of her had stung, and yet, she knew it had to do with him, not with her. She wasn't sure why she was so certain of that, but she was. "I can't regret it. It was a lot more about me than it was you, by the way, so maybe take some comfort in that."

A shadow passed through his eyes, intense, dark. But be-fore she could analyze it, it was gone.

A high-pitched wail shattered the moment. "Ah," Paige said. "There she is. It's a little past time for that."

She looked at him, and his total, casual nudity, and down at her blanket-covered breasts. "This is a little different now," she mused.

"What is?"

"Uh, the idea of being naked in front of you. When I was turned on things were a bit more hazy. Also, the room was darker. And I wasn't irritated with you."

"You're irritated with me now?"

She nodded. "Yes. I'll get over it, but for now, yes."

He nodded. "I'm going to shower now, so, you're safe." He turned and strode into the bathroom and she watched his butt the whole way, until he closed the door behind him.

Oh, he was so hot. And yes, that was maybe shallow. And yes, she was angry at him, which was just an even-greater testament to that hotness. But he was like four-alarm-fire hot, and she'd had sex with him. It was hard not to feel a little bit of smug triumph over that.

Sure, he hadn't gathered her into his embrace and held her all night long, but Dante had never promised romance. And she wasn't going to forget that.

She slipped out of bed over to the closet, grabbing a pair of sweats and a T-shirt, dressing as quickly as possible, doing a victory hop-step down the hall to Ana's room.

A little ray of joy broke through everything else when she saw Ana in her bed, kicking her feet, her eyes bright, her expression indignant. The memories, the confusion over Dante, for a moment, it all lessened.

"Morning, baby!" She leaned over and plucked her from her crib, kissing her soft head. "Let's go get breakfast."

She carried Ana downstairs and set her in her bouncy chair, letting her watch as Paige got her bottle ready. Then Paige picked her up and sat in one of the kitchen chairs to feed Ana. She smiled at the contented look on her face. Her fists were balled up by her face, her eyes round.

"Okay, take a break." Paige pried the bottle from Ana's lips, which earned her an indignant squeal. Then she propped her up over her shoulder and patted her back until she burped.

"Now you can have the rest." She returned her to her feeding position.

"My housekeeper isn't in on the weekend," Dante said when he entered the room.

"That's fine. I can pour a bowl of cereal. What do you usually do?"

"I can pour a bowl of cereal," he said.

"But you didn't even know if you had chocolate, so I assume you don't."

"I go out," he said.

"Ah."

"I take it you don't want to?"

"You can," she said. "I want to stay home with Ana. Spend more time on the terrace. She really liked it out there and it looks like it's going to be a beautiful day."

"I can pour a bowl of cereal," he said. "I can pour two. We can eat together."

He made it sound like he was submitting to mild torture. "You don't have to."

"It's the right thing," he said.

"Why? You think it's what you have to do because I was a virgin?"

"Yes. Don't protest. I've never slept with a virgin before. Allow me to salve my conscience."

"Bleah," she said. "Don't let your conscience be wounded on account of my hymen."

"*Dio*, Paige," he said, pulling a bowl out of the cupboard and slamming it onto the counter. "Must you say things like that?"

"I'm a blurter. I blurt. That's how we got into this situation in the first place."

"I remember."

"I thought you might. It's one of those defining moments in one's life. When someone lies about being engaged to you and you read about it in the news."

"That does stay with you."

She looked down at Ana. "You think I'm capable of taking care of Ana, right? Or being a mother, and seeing that she grows into a functional, happy human being?"

"I've said as much."

"Great. So why would you think I can't handle this?"

"I…"

"Exactly. You have no grounds. Either I'm tough enough to raise a child and fight to keep her, or I'm too wimpy to know my own mind and can't be trusted to make decisions about who I sleep with. But I can't be both."

"You could never be accused of being a wimp."

"Didn't think so. It would be like accusing you of being too effervescent."

He took a box of cereal out of the pantry. "You don't think I am?"

"No offense, but no."

"What am I then?" he asked.

Yet again, she could sense a strange, underlying seriousness to the question. And she had to wonder if sleeping with him had formed some sort of deeper connection, or if sex just made him philosophical.

"I'm not sure," she said. "Whatever you are, you're good underneath all that hardness on the outside."

"You think so?" he asked, a humorless smile curving his lips.

"I know so."

"How?"

"Here I sit in your kitchen, with Ana. And you're helping us. No matter how many layers of self-serving motivation you wrap it in, that's still the heart of it."

"I was paid back in full last night, don't you think?" His tone hardened, his eyes turning to cool chips of coal.

"Okay, now you've gone from misguided gentleman to a-hole. Not sure what happened there."

He crossed to the table and set her cereal in front of her.

She looked up at him. "I want coffee." Caffeine just might make this morning, and him, bearable.

"I don't make coffee."

"Oh, for the love of…" She stood up. "Hold her, please."

He looked stricken, his face frozen. "Hold her?"

"So I can make coffee, so we don't have to figure out a way to mainline the grounds directly into my bloodstream."

He took a step back, his expression closing off slowly, his black eyes going flat. "Let's go out."

"What?"

"All of us. It will make a nice photo-op for the press, don't you think?"

"I…suppose so."

"Why don't you go and get ready," he said.

"Okay." She stood from her chair and held Ana close as she made her way out of the kitchen and up to her room.

And that was when she realized that it had been her request for Dante to hold Ana that had triggered his idea of going out. And that in all the time since they'd come to live at his house, Dante had never once touched Ana.

After breakfast, Dante had spent the day in his office, working, avoiding Ana and Paige to the best of his ability. But it was impossible when they seemed to be everywhere. On his deck, in the living room. Paige's clothes were in his closet.

He stood from his desk and stalked out of the office, walking down the hall. He would go out and get some air. It was late and the lights were off in the house. Everything was quiet, blessedly so.

He walked down the stairs and to the living room, headed out toward the deck. And stopped cold. Paige was there, cradling Ana, who was wrapped in a blanket, in her arms.

He could hear her, singing softly, even through the closed doors.

It all came into focus slowly, and for a moment, he couldn't move, couldn't breathe. Paige smoothed Ana's hair with her hand, her expression so loving, so serene.

It choked him. Pain rose up in him, tightening its hold on him. Memories of another lullaby. Of his mother.

He loosened his tie, trying to get breath, clawing at the button on his shirt collar. He felt surrounded, crowded. Like nothing was his own anymore. Like his control was being pried from his hands.

He walked away from the scene, taking the stairs two at a time. He threw his bedroom door open, feeling his hold on his emotions, on his control, slipping from his grasp.

He turned and hit the wall with his open fist. It wasn't enough. It didn't take away from the explosion of feeling in his chest. He drew his arm back and punched the wall, pain biting into his skin, a dent in the plaster, a smear of blood on the paint that had been perfect and white a moment ago. He looked at his hand and dropped it back to his side, his eyes on the damage he had done.

Damage that he couldn't simply wash away. He could have someone come and fix it, of course, but that wasn't the point.

He stood there for a long time and simply looked. At what he had done. At the evidence of what happened when he lost his control.

Then he went into the bathroom and ran cold water over his stinging knuckles, focusing on the pain, on this consequence. Letting it overtake the suffocating emotion that had risen up inside of him. Letting it bring back his clarity of mind.

He needed space. He would spend the night in his office in the city. Anything to get away from this scene of domestic bliss. The vision of the kind of love that had been torn from him so many years ago.

Just a little space. That was all he needed. And he would be back in control.

CHAPTER ELEVEN

ANA was finally asleep, at eleven-thirty, and Paige was avoiding Dante. Which seemed pointless in some ways, as he'd been avoiding her since breakfast yesterday.

After they'd eaten, he'd disappeared into his home office. And then last night he'd disappeared completely, leaving a quick note saying he'd had a work emergency he'd had to go in for. At ten-thirty on a Saturday night. And today, she'd hardly seen him at all.

She'd spent time on the deck with Ana and a canvas, painting bold, brash colors that had nothing to do with the scene in front of her.

The ocean was too serene and beautiful. And nothing inside of her felt serene.

And now, Dante was in his home office, and she wasn't sure if, when she saw him again, he would be rude, or if he would get all "I have deflowered you and must make amends" again. If he would want her. Or if he would leave the house rather than face sleeping with her again.

She rolled her eyes and tiptoed down the stairs, headed for the kitchen and the rest of the chocolate ice cream.

She opened the freezer and let the cool air wash over her face. She felt confused. And lonely. She didn't know why the loneliness was hitting so hard now. When Shyla had died, it had been hard. So very hard. But Ana needed her. Ana had needed her from that moment and every moment since then and there had been no time to dissolve.

There was still no time to dissolve. And in the absence of total dissolution, perhaps there could be an ice-cream binge and a few tears.

"I was looking for you."

She turned and closed the freezer, forgetting the ice cream. Dante was there, looking end-of-the-day rumpled. Which for Dante meant he'd discarded his jacket and had obviously run his hands through his hair a few too many times. Otherwise, he remained well pressed, his black tie in place, his white shirt tucked into white slacks. She had the overwhelming urge to ruffle him.

To really find the man beneath the layer of rock and stone he kept around himself. To find out who he really was.

She'd seen glimpses of it. When he spoke of his mother. When he'd expressed genuine concern for her well-being after they'd slept together. And in each of those moments, there had been so much. Tenderness, love even, when his mother had been mentioned. But also a haunting sadness and fear that tore at her insides.

The fear she saw when he looked at her and Ana. Dark, endless. She wished she could watch it for a moment, to try to understand it. But he always covered it too quickly, taking control again as soon as he could.

She felt compelled to seek it out. Compelled to unbury it all. The good, the ugly. She had a feeling she could never reach the good if she didn't uncover the bad, too. Expose it to the sunlight.

A few days ago, she would have rejected the idea. Because Ana was her world. And Ana was still her world. But Dante was starting to be a huge part of it, too. Not a separate part, or a bigger part, or even a smaller part. He was folded in. Impossible to extricate.

And that was just damned terrifying.

"I figured you had lots more work to do. Since it's Satur-day and you put on a tie."

"I work, Paige. It's what I do."

"And what do you do for fun?"

He took a step closer to her. "I can think of one thing."

Her heart slammed into her chest. "Oh, well, yeah. Eating chocolate ice cream is what you mean, right?" She turned back to the freezer trying to defuse some of the tension be-tween them. Because, given her recent realization, she was more than happy to defer any intensity between them.

"Not quite."

Dante watched Paige's valiant effort to ignore him by dig-ging through the freezer for much longer than necessary. She was probably making the smart choice, denying the fire that ignited between them.

He'd tried to do it all day. Work punctuated by push-ups, bicep curls until he was sure his arms were going to drop out of their sockets. Anything to build enough pain to block out the intense need that had been rioting through him from the moment he'd gotten out of bed the other night and left her there alone, when he'd wanted nothing more than to take her again. And again. And again.

He wanted even more to try to eradicate the pain in his chest that seemed to hit him, so hard and strong whenever he looked at Paige holding Ana. A mother and her child. The love that passed between them. The truest love he'd known. The love he had lost.

He wanted to crush those feelings. Bury them beneath something stronger. Lust. Sex. Desire.

Yes, Paige was being the wise one.

And for once, he wasn't. Couldn't be.

He moved behind her and put his hand on the freezer door. She froze in front of him, her petite frame stiff.

"Don't ignore me, Paige," he said. He swept her hair to the side and bent, pressing a kiss to the side of her neck. "Ever."

She shivered beneath his touch. "I wasn't."

"You were trying to ignore this—" he traced the line of her neck with the tip of his tongue "—and you know we can't."

"I don't know. Maybe I don't know, because I'm just so gosh darn innocent."

He put his hands on her waist, drawing her backside up against his growing erection. "Don't make a joke of this. Don't put distance between us."

"I… Okay."

"I've had the day to think about it and the conclusion I've come to is that yes, you were a virgin. But you were right—you knew what you were doing. And you certainly seem to know what you want. So, let me ask you now, what do you want?"

"Ice cream," she said.

"Too sticky." He reached past her and took an ice cube out of the bin that sat in the back of the freezer, the chill burning his fingertips before it started to melt. "This, on the other hand, has some possibilities."

He held the ice cube above her shoulder, a drop of water hitting the curve of her neck and rolling down her pale skin. He leaned in and followed the trail of the drop with the tip of his tongue, warming the cold places.

She put her hands on the fridge, as if bracing herself.

"Good?" he asked.

"I would never have thought of that," she whispered. "So maybe I'm more innocent than I thought."

He pressed the corner of the ice cube to her neck, then removed it, following up with a hot kiss. "Do you want me to stop?"

He felt like he was poised on a razor's edge, waiting for her answer, watching the rise and fall of her petite shoulders with each intake of breath. He would stop if she asked. He would.

"No," she whispered. "Don't stop."

Relief flooded him, the sweeping intensity of it pulling on something inside of him. Pulling something loose. The chains to his tightly bound control fell and he felt, for the first time, a kind of deep and growing intensity that he was certain could consume them both.

And he wanted it. Welcomed it. He wanted to drown in it. Lose himself completely.

Never in his life had desire felt like this. Lust was a focused thing for him. Find release, and satisfy it. But this wasn't about release. This was about the softness of Paige's body. About the cold, salt and heat in her skin.

This was about the way it would feel to slide inside her again. So tight and perfect.

This was about the journey. About making it take as long to get to the destination as possible.

"I was hoping you would say that." He gripped the hem of her shirt and she helped him tug it up over her head. Then he turned her, shutting the freezer behind her.

Her round blue eyes were focused on him as she unhooked her bra, revealing those small, perfect breasts to him. Her nipples were puckered, from arousal, from the cold.

He placed the ice cube on her collarbone, water spilling down as he let it drift over her flesh, the droplets curving over the shape of her breasts, tightening her nipples even further, changing them to a deeper shade of blush.

He leaned down and ran his tongue over her breast, then sucked the tightened bud between this lips, the taste of her sending a jolt of painful need through him, making his shaft pulse, the ache in his stomach intensify.

She arched into him, her back against the door of the refrigerator. He continued to suck her breast, one hand anchored on her hip, the other directing the ice, leaving drops on her stomach that rolled downward. She squirmed, a sharp moan of pleasure on her lips.

"Good," he said, his lips still at her breast.

"Yes," she whispered.

He straightened and touched the ice to her lips, then kissed her there, deeply. Her lips were cold, the inside of her mouth, her tongue, hot.

He'd never imagined a sexual game could be exciting. He'd never played a sexual game, because sex had never been about the journey.

Until now.

He pulled his mouth from hers and she looked at him, her lips parted. He slipped the remaining bit of ice cube into her mouth, letting it melt on her tongue.

She leaned in and pressed her cold lips to his throat, the tip of her icy tongue tracing a line on his skin. Cold had long been a method he'd used to regain a handle on his emotions. Of stopping himself from getting out of hand. Of forcing his mind blank, effecting a reboot.

But this wasn't cooling him. It was heating him, burning him from the inside out, the chill on his skin evaporated by the heat running through his veins.

Paige turned and opened the freezer again, producing her own ice cube, a wicked grin on her face. She separated the top four buttons on his shirt and pressed the ice to his chest. Burning cold assaulted him, but it did nothing to cool the fire that was streaking through his body.

He was shaking, his entire body in pain with the need to free himself and sink into her. To be joined to her. Lost in her. To find the ultimate heat and burn alive in it.

He pushed her back against the fridge, every last ounce of his control gone. He pressed her hand against his chest, letting the ice burn, then numb, melting against his skin as he kissed her lips, as he devoured her.

She freed her hands and reached around behind him, tugging his shirt up out of his pants and unbuttoning it quickly, shrugging it off his shoulders and leaving it on the ground. And he didn't care.

He pushed her pajama pants down, along with her panties—the panties that proved just how little she'd expected to be having another sexual encounter with all their sensible cottonness—and kicked them to the side. He reached around, cupped her butt and lifted her so that her legs were wrapped around his waist, her arms around his neck.

He moved, turning them both, and pinning her against the wall. He used one hand to open his belt, undo his slacks and jerk his pants partway down, releasing his erection and sliding it through her moist folds.

She tightened her hold on him, her fingernails biting his skin, sharp pain piercing his flesh, ramping up his need.

"*Dio*, yes." He slid inside of her, her body hot around him, perfect. So wet and sweet. He thrust up hard and she gasped, blue eyes opening wide. "Okay?"

She bit her lip, nodding. She was so perfect. So very Paige. There was no woman like her anywhere, no woman who had ever made him feel this way.

And then there was no thought. There was only feeling. Burning in his chest and lungs, tightness in his gut, the pressure of impending release, building, building until he was certain he would burst with it. He gritted his teeth, tightening his hold on her hips as he thrust hard into her.

She let her head fall back against the wall, a strangled cry on her lips, her internal muscles pulsing around him, heightening his own need.

Finally, he gave in, pushing into her one last time, orgasm exploding through him, pleasure that was almost pain curling itself around every muscle, every vein, overtaking his entire body as he spilled himself inside of her.

His thighs shook, trembled. He set her down, making sure her feet were planted firmly on the floor before letting himself sink to his knees in front of her, his hands braced on the wall.

He put his head down, trying to catch his breath, trying to clear his mind. He felt full, and completely drained at the same time. Weak, depleted. In need. But there was no room for anything else in him, nothing but the intensity of the desire that was still ignited in his chest, in his bones.

He pushed away from the wall, away from her, and stood.

"I'm going to shower," he said. He had to escape. Had to put distance between them. As much as he'd needed it after the first time, he needed it more now.

He turned and walked away from her, leaving her there, naked against the kitchen wall, regret clinging to him like a film on his skin.

When he got to his bathroom, he turned the water on cold and put himself directly under the spray, trying to ease the feeling. To numb himself inside and out. He put his hand on the tiled wall and leaned forward, struggling to catch his breath beneath the icy assault.

Cold that would normally have wiped his mind clean, now made him think of the ice cube on his chest, followed by the warmth of her hands, her lips, her…

He had been out of his mind. Absolutely and completely. She had done it to him, had pushed him past the point of return. And he knew better. He *knew*.

For every loss of control there was a cost. He had lost his control. He had taken her without a condom. Without any consideration for how innocent she really was. For how sweet she was. For the fact that she wasn't the kind of woman you pinned to the wall and screwed.

He hit the tile with his fist, the stone hard beneath his hand, the grout biting into his flesh. He did it again. And again. Again until the pain shot up his arm, burned in his shoulder, left the skin on his fist raw, bleeding.

Nothing blacked out the pleasure that was still moving through him. Stronger than the regret. Stronger than the punishment.

So he lowered his head, and let the water wash over him. And waited. Waited for it to wash his feelings away.

Paige managed to collect her clothes and eat a bowl of ice cream. She was a little too stunned to face Dante. He had done…he had done things to her that she'd never imagined in her wildest fantasies. And she'd done things to him she'd never...

Oh, boy.

And then he'd left. And she didn't know why. Reasons, reasons she made up, were buzzing around in her head, but they probably weren't true, or they were at least only true in part. Dante wasn't an easy man to figure out and she knew she wasn't going to do it in five minutes over a bowl of Rocky Road.

She stood up and put the bowl in the sink, then made her way up the stairs. Ana was still sound asleep, completely unaware of the disaster that the two adults in the house were making of everything. And Paige had a choice to make: her room, or Dante's room?

Yes, they had said they would do this while she lived here. But if his behavior after their first time was an indicator, he didn't really want to share her bed.

Well, he was going to have to meet her in the middle. She wasn't having sex with him and then creeping back to her own room like they were sneaking around. She just wasn't. Yes, she did want to keep her heart uninvolved, and yes, she did fear that in some ways it was too late. But still. She wanted what she wanted, and he would have to deal with it.

Granted, she wasn't an expert but she felt like falling asleep next to each other was an essential piece of the sex equation. She also felt a new surge of confidence, one she'd never felt before. He wanted her. He desired her. That meant she had some negotiating power here.

She walked into Dante's room without knocking, and saw that he wasn't in it. She could hear the water running in the bathroom, but there was no cloud of steam. No extra warmth from what, by her quick calculations, had to have been a thirty-minute shower.

She walked into the bathroom, her hands shaking a little bit.

"Dante?"

He didn't answer. There was nothing, only the sound of the water.

"Dante," she said, this time more forceful.

She pulled open the shower door and her heart stopped. Dante was standing, his hands braced on the wall, his head down, as water, cold water, rained down on his back. His muscles were shaking, his skin bright red.

"What are you doing?" she asked, certain she didn't want to know. But equally certain that she had to know.

He lifted his head, his expression blank, his lips gray, his eyes black, bottomless pools. A shiver racked his frame.

Paige jolted into motion, grabbing a towel off the rack and holding it out to him. "Get out of there."

"It didn't work," he said, his tone dark, a tremor running through his words.

"What didn't work? You didn't freeze your balls off yet?" she snapped. "Come here."

"You have to pay for it somewhere, Paige," he said, his tone rough, unsteady. "Every ounce of pleasure has a price."

Her heart curled in on itself. He didn't make any sense to her, but the undertone to his words was so raw, so very serious. She might not understand his words, but he did. And they carried a weight that she feared could crush them both.

She put her hand on his back, on his ice-cold skin. "A little bit of cold is sexy, but this isn't." She draped the towel across her arm and planted her hands on his shoulders, tugging on him. It wasn't her strength that got him out of the shower, it was the fact that he complied.

He didn't feel like himself. He was usually solid, hot beneath her fingertips. The muscle beneath his ice-cold skin trembled now, his stance weak. And his eyes…they weren't blank now. The anguish was evident, there for her to see, to examine like she'd wanted. And now, she wanted to look away, because the rawness of it was simply too much. The pain too great.

But she didn't. She met his gaze as she brushed the towel

over his skin, drying him, her hands trembling, her stomach sick. "Come on. Let's go to bed."

He complied again, following her into the bedroom and sliding between the covers.

Paige stripped her clothes off and got in beside him, pushing her breasts against his freezing-cold back, wrapping her arms around him as he shivered against her.

A tear rolled down her cheek and she pressed her face to his shoulder blade. "You're so cold," she said.

"That's the idea," he said, his voice stronger now.

"Why?"

"A habit, I suppose."

"You take cold showers after sex?"

"No. Not so simple. I pay penance."

"For what?" she asked, trying to keep the horror from her tone. "For sins?"

"For feeling. For losing control. I've used it to train myself." His tone was flat, lifeless.

"Why?" she asked, her voice barely a whisper.

"Because, *cara mia*, nothing in life is free. Everything has a cost. Especially deep emotion. Most especially passion. Life is made of light and dark, good and bad. The other side of love is hate, and the line between the two is thin."

"I've never thought so," she said. "I don't think love and hate are anywhere near each other."

"And that's where you're wrong." He shivered again. "Because you haven't seen it turn. But I have. I told you about my mother. That she died. That I remembered her soft touch, and her singing. But I also remember how she died. How she was killed. My father killed her. While I watched from behind the couch, helpless to do anything but cover my ears to block out the sound. I will never forget what it's like to watch someone die. My mother. My own mother. I won't forget holding her in my arms as she faded. That's what happens when you have no control. When you are ruled by passion. That's what it can become. And that's why I remind myself that when you lose control, someone pays."

She tightened her hold on him, more tears sliding down her cheeks. "Why do you have to pay, Dante?" They were the only words she could voice. There were so many words she wanted to say. So many. And they weren't enough. They never would be.

"So no one else will."

She just held him then, her eyes stinging, her entire body, down to her soul exhausted. But she couldn't sleep. So she held him, warming him, until the darkness faded and light started to invade the room.

If only she could find a way to do the same for him. To shine a light on his soul and banish the darkness.

CHAPTER TWELVE

"WE'RE moving the wedding up to a week from yesterday."

Dante strode into her office midway through the day on Tuesday, a strange sight considering he had ignored her all day Monday and then had gone out to the office after hours on Monday night and not come home.

She'd driven Ana and herself to Colson's that morning, and she was still more than slightly peeved at him over the disappearing act.

She knew why he'd done it. The phrase running scared seemed a nice way to describe it. Still, she'd been imagining him dead on the side of the road. She'd called, but he hadn't answered, and pride prevented her from doing it more than five times. So she'd paced the hall instead. And she'd gone to sleep in his bed, inhaling the scent of him on his pillow, because it turned out that sex made her feel somewhat mushy about a guy.

"You can't reschedule what was never scheduled," she said, dryly, her heart hammering. "And that's way too soon."

"No, it's not. It's time we got everything going. I'm not running a bed-and-breakfast."

His words were like a slap to the face. "Right. Oh, my mistake. That's what I thought I was doing at your house. In my defense you shouldn't have put a little check-in desk with a bell right by the front door."

"Paige…"

"Dante," she said, her tone mocking.

"You know what I meant."

"You're being an insulting bastard. Is that what you meant? Because if that was the aim, great job. You did it."

"I meant this isn't permanent."

"Yeah, I do know that. You keep reminding me of it, actually."

"Do you want to get the adoption finalized as soon as possible or would you like to continue with your wounded maiden routine?" he asked.

"The adoption."

"I thought so."

"So we're getting married on Monday and…and what's with the adoption?"

"I have made a very generous donation to the local child services department. They like me a lot. I'm imagining that the rest of the process should go off without a hitch."

"You…bought the adoption?"

"More or less. But I imagine if they found something terrible about us they wouldn't allow it."

"That's…oh, that just makes me so mad!" She stood up and kicked a box of decorations aside. "I had to work so hard to prove I was fit, all because I was single and lived in a small apartment or whatever, and you waltz in with your—sorry, but it's true—bad reputation, but oh, you have money, so no problem let's get this adoption show on the road."

"I'm sorry you're frustrated but I imagine the relief of knowing it will be finalized soon will take the sting out of it."

She covered her mouth and sat on the edge of her desk. "Oh, you're right. Oh…she's really going to be mine." She popped up and took two leaping steps toward him and threw her arms around him. "Thank you so much."

He just stood, stiff, unmoving.

She stood up on her tiptoes and brushed a kiss to his cheek. "No glitter today," she whispered.

He pulled away from her. "That's good."

"Will your parents be at the wedding?" she asked.

He paused, his jaw hardening. "They'll have to be invited. I don't…I would rather not lie to them."

"I don't want anyone to know," she said. "And I know maybe it's selfish, but if anything were to jeopardize my getting Ana…"

"I understand," he said, his voice firm.

"And I understand why you don't want to lie to them. They're your parents and…"

"Yes. They are."

"They were good to you, weren't they?" He always spoke of them so formally, no warmth in his tone.

"Yes," he said. "Very. They gave me firm guidance, which I needed desperately. Gave me everything I needed. My own space, which I never had before. My own things."

She'd noticed how meticulously he cared for everything, and suddenly, she realized why. He had been in foster care for around eight years and that had likely meant a lot of moving, and owning very little.

"Love?"

He shrugged. "I don't need that."

The statement shocked her, even though, after the other night, it probably shouldn't. "But…don't they?"

His expression froze. "I…it's not that I don't…"

But he couldn't say it, or think about it really, she could see that. "I know. And I'm sure they know."

"They'll probably enjoy a wedding far too much. Though I'm not sure what they'll think about one on notice this short."

"I'm sure they'll be fine with it."

"I'm sure Mary will pitch a fit about finding a mother of the groom dress on such short notice." The ghost of a smile touched his lips.

"Well, yeah, but most women would."

"There's something else I need to say."

An apology maybe? That would be nice. She would happily take an apology.

"What?"

"I didn't use a condom the other night."

Her stomach sank a little. Not an apology. "Oh."

"I need to know if you're pregnant. I'll need you to tell me."

She nodded. "I would. I will."

For a moment, she was afraid her knees might give out. What would she do if there was a baby? What would it mean for Ana? For the adoption? Would she be a single mother of two children? She wasn't entirely certain she could handle one. The idea of juggling both…it terrified her.

"Good."

"I'm not, though," she said, because she had to believe it. The alternative was too frightening. Another example of her taking something that was working and making an impossible jumble out of it.

"You don't know that."

"Dammit, Dante, I have to believe I'm not."

He laughed, a humorless sound. "I don't blame you for not wanting my baby. You've heard about everything lurking in my gene pool. Hell, I've treated you to a front row seat."

"That's not it," she said, ice trickling through her veins. "But be honest with me. If I were, would you even stay? Or would I be on my own with two children?"

"You would be better off without me."

"I suppose that answers my question."

"Sadly, it doesn't. I would stay. But it's better you don't need that. Better I don't have to."

"I don't want to be someone you're forced to be with."

"If you're having my baby, then you will be. I will take care of my responsibilities, make no mistake."

Her stomach tightened. He looked…resigned. She didn't want that. Not for the rest of her life. "You would…you would love our child wouldn't you?"

"I don't think I could."

"You don't mean that. You just…you need to put the past behind you and…and…"

He exploded then, a dark flame in his eyes burning bright, stealing the light from the room. "Look around you, Paige. I own all of this. Things have already happened for me. What do you think, that I need to talk about my feelings? That I need a psych? To what? To listen to me? Because that will fix it? That will bring my mother back? It will make it so I don't share half my blood with a violent killer? Is that it? It will fix me. Make me happy and able to love?" He shook his head. "You live in fairyland. But the real world has less glitter. You can't fix everything."

"Dante that's not… I'm not trying to trivialize…"

"You did. I have a business trip that I need to go on this week. I'll be back in time for the wedding. Everything is being planned. All we have to do is show up."

"You're leaving?"

"I have business," he bit out.

"Fine." She went back to her desk and sat behind it, her heart in her throat. She had no idea where they stood. Except that they were both angry at each other. And that he was leaving while still angry at her. But she couldn't figure out how to fix it, even though she hated it.

He walked to her desk quickly and braced his hands on the surface, leaning in and taking her mouth in a hard, intense kiss. She was lost in it, in him, the moment his lips touched hers. She pushed her fingers through his hair, slid her tongue against his.

He pulled away, straightening. Dark and dangerous. "When I get back, we'll have the wedding. Then we'll have the wedding night."

The media had often accused Dante of atrocious behavior, and very often it had been a part of the myth they'd spun around him for their own enjoyment.

This time, with no witnesses other than Paige, he would have deserved it.

But his world was ordered, well controlled, just as he needed it and she seemed bound and determined to come in and challenge him at every turn.

He didn't know why he'd told her so much about his mother. About why he took cold showers, and hit things. It sounded crazy when voiced, and maybe in some ways it was. But it had been necessary. The way he'd controlled his emotions as a young boy moving around in the foster system. Anger had to have a release, but if he gave the consequence to himself, no one got hurt. It had flooded over into every emotion until it had been easy to simply not have them.

He hadn't needed the intense, physical reminder for years. Not until Paige came into his life.

Even with those precautions, everything had crashed down around him. He might have gotten her pregnant. A child. His child. He wasn't the man for that. He couldn't even look at Paige and Ana without being taken over by memories of his mother. Couldn't bear to touch the child because she reminded him too much of what it was to be so helpless.

And he couldn't, wouldn't allow himself, to imagine what it would be like to have a child of his own. To share his poisoned blood. The blood he shared with his father. The blood he worked so hard to keep under control.

He was failing. He had failed, in every way that mattered.

And Paige might be the one to pay for it. Someone always paid. Paige. Ana. The child, if there was one. All tied to him because of an act of carelessness.

The truth was, this business trip could be deferred. But he had to get his control back. He had to get distance.

And as long as Paige was around, as long as he had to see her, with her petite curves and tendency to dress in sequins, to listen to the sound of her voice, that voice that he'd heard moaning with pleasure, as long as he had to smell that sweet

floral scent combined with the fresh smell of her clean skin...
he wouldn't be able to master his emotions.

And he had to. There was no other option.

Even if it might already be too late.

Midnight, the day of the wedding, Dante arrived back at his
San Diego home. It had been a long trip. And his bed had
seemed cold, empty.

He had made promises, threats, really, about a wedding
night, but he had no doubt Paige wouldn't be too thrilled if
he tried to make that happen. And he wouldn't blame her.
He'd acted like an ass to her.

About everything. About the potential baby.

But he had everything contained now. One thing the time
away had been good for was to start feeling like himself
again. To start feeling like he had some semblance of control
over his mind and body.

Whatever was ahead for them, they would handle. So long
as he maintained his distance, in an emotional sense, everything would be fine.

He walked into the house, expecting silence, and heard
Ana's indignant wailing instead. He walked up the stairs,
toward her room, expecting Paige to be there as she'd been
their first night together.

But she wasn't there.

He could hear the water running in the next room. Paige
was in the shower, and since it was the time when Ana was
normally asleep, she was probably stealing what had been
her first chance of the day.

But now the baby was crying. Deep sobs. A sound so sad,
so pitiful. And so full of helplessness that it called to him,
resonated in him.

He walked into the nursery, an image in his mind of a
small boy on the floor, crying endless tears, with no one there
to comfort him. Crying for a mother who would never return.
He approached Ana's crib, his heart pounding in his head.

He swallowed and looked down at her. "Why are you crying, *principesa*?"

She looked at him, her owlish eyes wide and furious, and continued bawling.

He reached out to her slowly, placing his hand flat on her round tummy. She quieted and wiggled beneath his palm, her expression morphing to one of curiosity. When he didn't satisfy it immediately, she started to cry again.

He could go and pull Paige out of the shower, which she had done to him. Of course, his had been a shower with a self-destructive bent, rather than one intended for cleanliness. Or he could handle this himself.

He couldn't remember if he'd ever held a baby before. He doubted if he had. But he had seen the way Paige held her, with infinite care and sweetness. Close to her body to keep her safe. And if...if his carelessness had resulted in a pregnancy, he would have to learn.

He bent forward and scooped her into his arms, pulling her up against his chest. The discomfort that bordered on fear whenever he saw Ana started to fade, replaced with that tenderness he always saw on Paige's face when she held her daughter. He didn't want to acknowledge it, that softening in his chest. But surely it was right to feel tender toward a baby? A sign that perhaps not everything in him was frozen.

Ana stopped crying, her heart beating fast like a little bird's as she nestled into his chest. "Is that all you wanted?" he asked, his voice breathless. "To be held?"

She melted into him, her little body supported by his hands. The trust she had in him humbled him, broke something deep inside of him.

She shifted, a sharp cry of discontentment on her lips.

He sat down in the rocking chair, hoping the back-and-forth movement would calm her.

Sing to her.

He remembered Paige asking him to do that the first night.

I don't know any lullabies.

A lie.

Ana wiggled against him, her crying becoming more insistent.

He took a deep breath, moving his hand over her back. For a moment he could not force the words out. They stuck in his throat, stuck, along with the image in his mind of the little boy curled up on the floor. That was the last time he had sung the song. The last time he had let the words out.

He moved his hand over Ana's back, felt her warmth. Her breath. Her life. She was not cold. She was not gone.

She would hear the song. She would take comfort in it.

He took a breath. *"Stella stellina, la notte se avvicina."* She quieted at the sound of his voice, her wide eyes trained on his face. His chest felt tight, his throat threatening to close, but he kept on. Up until the end. *"Nel cuorre della mamma."* *And all are sleeping in the mother's heart.*

Ana rested her head on his chest, relaxed her body against him. And he put his cheek on top of her feather-soft head.

"Papa's heart, too," he said, without thinking.

His own words jolted him back to reality. Ana didn't have a father. He certainly couldn't fill that place in her life. He couldn't fill the place at Paige's side, either. A husband. A father. He wasn't meant to be either of those things.

He had nothing in him to give. A few moments in a rocking chair, a song, didn't change that. He was bound up too tight, everything in him ordered, set, unable to be moved. If he opened up at all, if he changed one thing, he was afraid it would all collapse. Afraid that his control would slip. That the pain, the ugliness, that lived in him would be unleashed on the innocent people around him.

That couldn't happen. Not ever.

Still, he stayed, in this moment outside of reality. A quiet moment, the kind a man like him had never been given before. To hold someone so helpless, so precious, who trusted him so completely for no other reason than that life had always handed her people who cared for her. Because she had never been touched by someone who intended evil.

He wasn't the kind of man who prayed, but in that moment, he prayed that she never was.

CHAPTER THIRTEEN

IT was her wedding day. Strange because she'd never given a lot of thought to her wedding day. Although, when her mind had wandered to the event she'd imagined—the very few times she'd imagined anything—a lot of color.

Glitter, naturally. Having some friends and family present, no matter how fraught the relationship, would have been nice, too.

But she'd opted out of it because she simply hadn't told her parents, or siblings, that she was engaged, so that made it easy.

And now, in her gorgeous but sedate satin gown, with her hair pinned up, so that her pink stripe was covered, as commanded by the hairdresser, she felt a little sad about her lack of support. About the fact that she hadn't put more of her own personal stamp on things.

Which was stupid, because this was a very temporary marriage to a man who meant nothing to her. A man who was just her boss. And who was just the most fascinating, interesting, sexy man she'd ever met. And who was, oh, yeah, also her lover.

So there was that, too, but it was still no big deal and not worth getting worked up over.

Too bad she was worked up.

She blamed some of the worked up on getting out of the

shower last night and finding Dante sitting in the rocking chair, holding Ana against his chest. Singing.

That had made something crack apart in her chest. Had left her feeling vulnerable, tender. Different.

She took a deep breath and bunched up handfuls of her slippery skirt. She didn't have time to get all moony. Ana was already in the church, with Genevieve who was acting as an attendant and babysitter. They'd opted to include Ana in the ceremony because, honestly, the party was for her. The whole thing was for her.

Paige hoped, sincerely, that Ana never doubted how loved she was. Because this was nothing, only a small piece of what she was willing to go through in order to secure her daughter's safety and happiness. In order to keep her in her life.

She would walk through fire. All today required was a corset and mascara. And some vows. In a church.

So maybe she *would* walk through fire for all this eventually.

At least now she felt equipped to do it. Felt like she had the strength. She didn't know what had happened to her over the past few weeks, but something in her had changed. She wasn't afraid that everything she touched would turn to sand and blow away in the wind. Wasn't afraid that she was destined to fail. She felt…powerful. Like she had the power to do what had to be done.

"Ms. Harper?" The wedding planner, the one who had thrown everything together at the last minute without batting an eye, poked her head into the waiting area Paige was standing in.

"Yes?"

"It's time to queue up."

Paige nodded and walked out of the quiet little entryway into the foyer of the church. Two wooden double doors loomed in front of her. She could hear people talking quietly, and she could hear music.

"Dante, Genevieve and Ana are already in place. You just wait until I signal you."

Paige nodded, unable to come up with any words.

Then, way too quickly, the wedding planner gave her the signal and the doors swung open. Paige took a deep breath and started to walk slowly down the aisle, her heart pounding in her head.

She didn't really like having everyone's eyes on her, because there was a very high likelihood of her tripping or otherwise making a fool out of herself, and she really didn't relish a thousand people bearing witness to her clumsiness.

One foot in front of the other.

She concentrated on that. On making it down smoothly. And she didn't once look up at Dante. She found Ana first, clinging to Genevieve, her frilly white dress bunching out around her, a headband with an oversize flower decorating her short hair.

Only at the end, when she had nowhere else to look, when it was time for her to take Dante's hand, did she look at him.

And it was like the whole sanctuary, the whole city, the whole world, cracked apart around her and fell away. He was beautiful, but he was always beautiful. The tuxedo highlighted the hard lines of his trim physique, the candlelight casting shadows in the hollows of his face, making his cheekbones sharper, his jaw more square.

But that wasn't it.

He took both of her hands and the pastor began the ceremony. She managed to say the vows, managed to repeat them when it was her turn, to keep from stumbling over her words.

But when the command was given to kiss the bride and Dante's lips touched hers, she realized what it was. And it filled her with a sense of bone-deep terror, and a kind of pure, intense elation that she'd never experienced before in her life.

Dante wasn't just her boss. He wasn't just a man who was helping her. He wasn't just her temporary husband. He wasn't even just her lover.

Dante was the man she loved. The only man she'd ever loved. The man who was worth the risk. The man who had made her fear of being unwanted seem like nothing. Because she was willing to fight for him. Willing to risk herself, her heart, for him.

Because she loved him.

And she knew that the admission would send him running back up the aisle alone.

So, she said nothing, and she kept on kissing him.

"And now I pronounce them, not only husband and wife, but a family," the pastor said.

Genevieve handed Ana to Paige and Paige took her, held her daughter close against her chest, her heart thundering, as Dante took her free hand.

"I am proud to present the Romani family."

Dante was grinning, the kind of grin designed to make the headlines. The kind of grin designed to impress child services. The kind that Paige knew was a fake. Because she could see the emptiness in his eyes.

She was finding it a little hard to fake it, considering the revelation that had just slapped her in the face.

She wasn't sure when it had happened, the love thing. When a crush had changed into something real, something deeper. Sometime in between when he'd stood in front of her desk like an avenging angel demanding an explanation, and when he'd cradled Ana against his chest and sang to her with the most profound tenderness she'd ever seen from him.

They walked down the aisle, to thundering applause, and she wondered, for the first time, who the people in attendance were. Friends of Dante's family. And friends of their friends, she imagined.

Paige forced a smile, and tried to keep a hold of Dante's hand. He leaned in, the motion likely seeming like an affection nuzzle to their audience. "Smile," he said.

"I am," she whispered back.

The double doors opened for them and they entered the empty foyer.

"You aren't," he said, once the doors closed behind them.

"Well, I'm not as good of an actor as you," she said.

He looked stricken by that statement and she couldn't understand why. It's what he was doing, she could tell.

"Well, you had best become better at it. We are headed to the reception now, and you are going to meet my parents."

Dante watched as Paige, pale and drawn, attempted to converse with guest after guest in the massive ballroom. He could tell she was fading. Ana had faded long ago, and was asleep in his arms, her face pressed hard against his shoulder.

Strange, how easy it was to get used to carrying the little girl, when he had avoided it for so long. It seemed natural now. Right.

Don and Mary, his mother and father by every right, caught his eye and made their way across the ballroom, their hands unlinked, but touching lightly with each step. They weren't overly affectionate and never had been. But they presented a strong front of solidarity. One that went well beyond a front, he was certain.

"Dante." Mary leaned in and pressed a kiss to his cheek, resting her hand on Ana's back. "We're so very happy for you."

He nodded, discomfort assaulting him. He hadn't wanted to lie to them. Not for anything.

Don smiled. "We were certain you'd never settle down, and then this. Out of the blue. Instant family. A granddaughter for us, too."

Guilt stabbed him. "A surprise for me, as well." That was the strict truth.

Paige looked over at him, and in moments she was flitting across the room. She came to his side, her hand on his arm.

"You must be Dante's parents," she said.

"And you're the world's most unexpected woman," Mary said. "We never thought Dante would choose family life."

"Ah, well," Paige said. "I sort of roped him into it. He didn't have a choice really."

Don and Mary laughed, because it sounded too ridiculous to be true. Even if it was. Though, that he'd had no choice was where Paige was wrong. He had a choice. He could walk away at any moment, but something was keeping him from doing it.

If only he knew what it was. Ana shifted against him, and a strange tightness invaded his chest.

"We do have a bit of a surprise for you," Don said. "Dante told us you weren't planning a honeymoon because of the baby. So Mary and I thought we would offer to take Ana for the night, and that we would send you to a hotel downtown."

Heat flooded through Dante's veins at the thought of a night alone with Paige. Not the best moment to be flooded with heat, all things considered. "One of your hotels?"

Don laughed. "Naturally."

"Oh," Paige said. "I don't know. I…"

Mary put her hand on Paige's. "I know you don't know us, but Dante does. And we're Ana's grandparents now. We want to be involved."

The statement made Paige look even more sallow than she had all day. "Right. Of course."

Dante handed Ana over to Mary, and Ana stirred, pinning her sleep-clouded eyes on the older woman. But she didn't shriek or make a fuss. That was one thing he found fascinating about Ana. She seemed to make instant assessments about people and then decide how to react according to that assessment.

In so many ways, she could have been his daughter. She was decisive. Focused.

The thought doused the fire that had been raging through him, killed it off with a streak of ice. She wasn't his daughter. She never would be.

Just like Paige wasn't really his wife. And they shouldn't

be. For their own sakes, it was a blessing they were not. And he could only hope that there would be no other child. That Paige wasn't pregnant.

He ignored the faint, treacherous feeling of hope that burned in him. The hope that she was. That he could keep her with him.

No. He would go on their mini honeymoon and enjoy their wedding night. But the fact that they'd signed a document didn't change anything. It didn't make any of it real. It didn't make any of it possible.

Forgetting that wasn't an option.

The suite was stunning. And Paige was shaking.

She'd hardly said two words to Dante for a week, and now they were going to get naked again, and have amazing sex, which was great. Except that sex with him had such a high cost to her emotions and while she was willing to pay it, she did have to gear up for it.

"That was very nice of your mom and dad," she said.

A muscle twitched in Dante's cheek. "It was."

"So this is your dad's hotel?" She knew he called his parents by their first names, but she felt awkward about it.

She walked across the sleek, modern room, to the window that provided a view of the lights in the Gaslamp Quarter. The city was glowing, still alive in spite of the late hour. And yet up in the top of the hotel, everything seemed so distant. Unreal.

It felt like an alternate reality up there. Both safer for its separation from the world and more dangerous for it.

She turned around to face Dante and her heart crumpled. He looked so perfect in his tux, his tie open, the top buttons on his shirt undone. He looked less than perfectly pressed for once. As if the day might have actually pierced that armor he valued so highly.

And she knew why now. She saw it clearly. What the press took as aloofness, a kind of unfeeling detachment, she knew

had been a survival technique. To protect the little boy who
had felt too much.

The boy whose world had broken before his eyes one horrible day, at the hands of the man who should have loved him.
Should have loved his mother.

She also saw, clearly, that Dante's parents loved him. That
Don and Mary had deep, real affection for the boy they'd
brought into their home as a teenager. And she saw that Dante
didn't realize it. That he kept himself from returning it, or at
least showing that he did.

Still protecting himself. Still guarding himself against
pain.

She recognized it clearly. It was a grand scale version of
what she'd done for most of her life. Don't care, don't hurt.
Don't try, don't fail.

"Champagne?" she asked, walking over to the full kitchen
area in the suite, touching the top of the bottle that was sitting
on ice, two crystal flutes set out for the newlyweds.

"Why not?" he asked. "It seems a traditional thing to do
on one's wedding night."

"Yes," she said. "And fitting, since you promised me the
rest of the night would be traditional, too."

He looked down, a lock of dark hair falling forward. "I
did. And I must apologize for that. For the way I treated you
before I left."

"I'm over it, Dante."

"Don't be," he said. "I behaved like an ass and I deserve
for you to be annoyed with me."

"I'm not, though. Since that first night with you I didn't
have any intention of going to bed alone on our wedding
night, so your demand was well in line with my plans."

He glowered at her, so serious and irritated she nearly
laughed at him. "You're impossible, Paige."

"Yeah, I've been told that." She took the champagne out
of the bucket and worked the cork, wincing when it popped
out. She poured two glasses and held one out to him. "I've

been told I'm quite impossible, in fact, but I never seem to change. And there was once a man who told me that maybe the problem isn't with me, but with other people."

He took the glass from her hand and held it up in salute, and she did the same.

"To your impossibleness," he said.

"I'll drink to that." She took a sip of the dry, bubbly liquid, her eyes never leaving his. "You know what's funny?"

"What?" he asked, leaning against the counter.

"The other times I've been called impossible…it wasn't because I was stubborn. Actually, I've spent my whole life being very, very not stubborn. I was impossible because I wouldn't apply myself. Because I never listened when my mother told me I should try harder. Or, rather because I stopped listening at a certain point."

"Explain."

"You know I'm going to. At length."

"Yes, I do know that about you."

"Anyway, the thing is, it became clear very early on that school was hard for me. My brother and sister, they were brilliant. My sister in academics, my brother in academics and in sports. They were stars. From day one they were like hometown heroes. My sister would go to national spelling bees and science fairs. My brother brought the high school football team to the state championships and scored the winning touchdown. My sister was the valedictorian of her graduating class."

She took another sip of her champagne and tried to stop the tears that were forming. It shouldn't hurt. Not after all this time.

"So then there was me. And I struggled to pay attention in class. To pull average grades. And it wasn't good enough. I was accused of not trying when I was. And I did try. I tried to do well. I tried to make friends and…and fit in. But it didn't work. And so I just…stopped. Because if I didn't care, then it didn't hurt so much. You remember I told you about the braces incident? That was another one of those moments. If I laughed with everyone else and made it a big joke, it was funny that I cut the hell out of a guy's tongue during my first kiss. If I could just laugh, when I got a flier handed to me in the halls that had a picture of me, covering my chest, with eggs on my face, well, then maybe I could be part of the joke instead of just being the butt of it. But I shut down inside. And I stopped trying."

Dante frowned, his dark eyebrows drawing together. "I have never looked at you and seen a woman who wasn't trying, Paige. Never."

"Not now," she agreed. "I've been changing, slowly over the past three years, since I moved. Since I got the job at Colson's and I saw that I could be really good at something other than just splashing paint on a canvas."

"People make a lot of money splashing paint on a canvas," he said drily.

"Yes, but I wasn't. And no one thought it had any kind of value, not in my family. Not in my community."

"Blind and stupid," he said, his tone harsh. "You have a gift for color and design. I still don't understand how they couldn't see it."

His anger on her behalf warmed her. Caused a little trickle of satisfaction to filter through her veins. But that wasn't why she was telling him about herself, about what she'd been through.

"And then there was Ana," she said. "Suddenly another person was depending on me caring. On me making a success. Throwing myself into it and not giving a thought to failure. Because I couldn't afford to think of failing. For Ana, it's been a pursuit of success at all costs and suddenly I realize that I can achieve things. With your help, I grant you. But..."

"But it was your bullheaded stubbornness that got me to help," he said.

"And that was something I didn't know I had." She looked into her drink, watched the bubbles rise to the surface as she picked her next words carefully. "But I had to be willing to stop trying to protect myself. I had to be willing to be hurt in order to grab anything worthwhile."

His expression flattened, light leaching from his dark eyes. "I'm happy you were able to do that."

So, he wasn't going to understand what she was saying. Or he was going to pretend that he didn't.

But she'd changed. And just because it wasn't easy, didn't mean she wasn't going to try. Because whether or not Dante ever loved her, Dante deserved to feel loved. He deserved to be healed. And he was worth any level of pain or disappointment she might face.

Because he was worth something. Everything.

Of all the realizations she'd had about Dante, the most terrifying, heart-wrenching one, was that her enigmatic, alpha boss, didn't see himself as valuable. He saw himself as a liability. As a roadblock to the happiness of others. As a danger, in many ways.

She would change that. No matter what happened between them in the end, she was determined to change that. She wasn't going to be the happy-go-lucky Paige Harper of three years ago. She wasn't even going to be the Paige she'd been a few weeks ago.

She was stronger now. She knew she had power. She knew she could succeed.

She set her glass on the counter, walked back over to the window, sensing Dante's gaze following her movements.

With the curtains open, the lights from the city casting a pale glow on the living area, Paige reached behind her back and gripped the tab on her zipper, sliding it down slowly, the fabric parting, exposing her back to the cool air.

The straps on the gown loosened, and she pushed them off her shoulders, the gown slipping down her body and pooling in a silken mass at her feet. She stepped away from it, keeping her back to him.

The strapless, lace undergarment she was wearing pushed

her breasts up high, contoured her waist, ending at her hips, just above the white, lace thong that barely covered anything. She left her stilettos on, bright pink and shocking, with glitter dusting the heels.

Confidence—unfamiliar, empowering—burned inside of her, along with a steady pulse of desire that beat a rhythm through her entire body, centered at the apex of her thighs.

"I can tell you something else I want," she said. "Something I'm determined to have."

"What's that?" he asked, his voice a low growl.

"You. Tonight, I'm going to have you."

"Do you think so?" His voice was closer now, feral. Arousing.

"I know it." She turned to face him, and the lean, hungry look on his face gave total evidence of her victory.

"My little innocent has become a seductress?"

"I always have been," she said. "I just needed to find her. She was always there. But you helped bring her out. Because you…knowing you, has changed me."

She could see it, clear and quick, a flash of fear in his eyes. "Have I?" he asked, his voice rough.

"Yes. You've helped me find my power. My peace with myself."

"How did I do that?" he asked.

"By being you."

She took a step toward him, her heart thundering, the need burning in her like fire overtaking any insecurity that might threaten to ruin the moment. Her moment. His moment.

She reached behind her back and started to undo the hooks and eyes on the corset bra, letting it fall to the floor, her breasts bare for his inspection.

He was watching her, motionless as stone, his body tense, his expression blank. But there was a wealth of information in that blank slate. She knew him well enough to know that now. That the less she saw, the more there was. The more desperately he was trying to hide. To keep control.

She wouldn't let him have it. Not tonight. She wanted more. More than their first night, more, even, than the night in the kitchen. She wanted it all. All of him.

She hooked her fingers in the sides of her panties and tugged them down her legs, kicking them to the side. Then she closed the distance between them, pressing her body against his, still fully clothed in his tux. She wrapped her arms around his neck and pressed a kiss to his lips.

"Handy thing about the high heels," she said. "I don't have to get up on my tiptoes. But I do think they leave me a little overdressed." She toed them off and shoved them out of the way. "And you are way overdressed."

Paige put her hands on his shirt and concentrated on undoing every last button, shoving it, along with his suit jacket, onto the floor.

"Relax, Dante," she whispered. "Don't you ever relax?"

"Show me a man who can relax while you're doing this to him. He does not exist." His voice was strangled, affected.

She planted her hand on his chest, feeling the heat of flesh and muscle beneath her palm. "I don't know very many women who could relax with you looking like this. I know I'm not exactly relaxed. Just incredibly turned on."

A groan escaped his lips and she captured it with hers, sliding her tongue over his, pressing her breasts to his bare skin. She pulled away from him, kissing his neck, tasting the salt of his skin, before traveling lower to his chest.

She traveled lower, lavishing attention on each ridge of muscle, his stomach contracting beneath her lips, his fingers tangling in her hair, working at the pins that held it in place.

She stopped at the waistband of his pants, tracing the line where flesh met fabric with the tip of her tongue. Then she started loosening his belt, pulling it slowly through the loops, watching the effect each movement had on her captive.

The muscles in his stomach jumped as her hand brushed the hardness of his cloth-covered erection, his eyes like black fire, burning into her, his attention rapt on her. There was no disinterest now. No flatness. Nothing veiled, nothing hidden.

She pushed his pants down his lean hips, leaving him gorgeous, naked and aroused for her exploration. She circled his length with her hand, testing the weight of him, the hardness. She squeezed him gently and earned a rough growl of pleasure. So uncivilized. So uncontrolled. So everything she wanted from him.

"I've been wanting to do this for a while," she said, on her knees in front of him, a subservient position. Ironic, because in that moment she knew, for a fact, that she was the one with all the power.

"What is that?" he asked. She could hear the strain in his voice, could hear the edge, how close he was to losing his control completely.

And she pushed. She leaned in, flicking her tongue over the head of his erection. Tasting him, testing him. So good. So perfect.

She dipped her head, taking him inside of her mouth, her lips sliding over his length. He pushed his fingers deeper into her hair, her curls falling out of the pins and cascading over her shoulders.

"*Dio*, Paige."

Her name on his lips was fuel for the fire. She continued to explore him with her mouth, her tongue, pushing him higher, harder. Pushing herself right along with him. She could feel him shaking, the muscles in his thighs, his hands in her hair unsteady.

"Enough," he said, his tone pleading. "I can't hold back."

And part of her didn't want him to. But another part, the selfish part that won, wanted to stop so that she could join him in release.

She pulled away from him, moving into a standing position, her eyes never leaving his. In the dim light, she could see the dull flush of arousal staining his high cheekbones, could see his chest rising and falling sharply with each labored breath.

Could see that she was close to uncovering the man beneath the armor.

"Come to bed with me," she said.

And he complied.

There were condoms in the bedside table, and Dante quickly rolled one on, joining her on the bed, stroking the silken seam between her thighs with his fingers, sliding a finger deep inside of her, testing her readiness.

"Oh yes," she breathed, the white-hot friction created by his touch sending a streak of pleasure through her each time he brushed his fingers over her clitoris.

"Ready for me?"

She bracketed his face with her hands, her eyes locking with his as she pressed a kiss to his lips. "Always," she said.

He slid inside of her, his eyes never leaving hers as he filled her, joined himself to her, in the most primal, basic, profound way possible.

This was why they called it becoming one. Because she couldn't tell anymore where he began and she ended. Couldn't tell whose pleasure she was feeling, whose desperation.

The need for release pounded through both of them, and each thrust of Dante's body within hers, each press of hers against his, brought them closer. She moved her hands over his back, felt the tension in his muscles, tension that echoed through her, tightened more and more, unbearably so.

He thrust hard into her one last time and pushed them both over the edge, a rough growl on Dante's lips.

She lay there, holding him against her body—her world, her defenses, at his feet. Somehow, it wasn't just about him anymore. It was about her. Not about breaking him down, but being broken in front of him. Of offering him everything, regardless of the consequences.

She ran her fingers through his hair, pressed a kiss to his shoulder. "I love you."

* * *

I love you.

It shouldn't matter how she felt. Ultimately, it changed nothing. It didn't alter the plans he'd been making, slowly, since the wedding. Since the moment she'd appeared at the church. Since he'd seen his parents with Ana.

What she felt changed nothing. On one thing, he was sure Paige was absolutely right: her love had no darkness to it. There was nothing in Paige but pure, beautiful light. And there was nothing more than that in her feelings.

She was all strength, determination and generosity.

He was the one who had to be kept on a leash. Of that he was certain. He had the blood of a monster in his veins. He had seen what love had done to that man. How he had let it get twisted inside of him. Love becoming about hurting someone else, controlling her, never controlling himself.

He would never do that. Would never allow it.

He had lost something of his control back in that bed with Paige, but he would not allow it to happen again. The feeling, though, with her, was proving addictive. The temptation to drown in passion, in her arms, was strong.

He gripped the rail of the balcony and looked out at the city below. The air was warm, but he was cold to his bones. There was no need for him to exact punishment on himself tonight, no need to remind himself of the destruction he was capable of.

I love you.

Paige loving him, what it might do to her, that was the cruelty. That was the punishment.

Maybe it's a good thing. Maybe it will keep her with you.

Not a kindness on his part, perhaps, but he had been considering it, strongly. To keep Paige and Ana in his life. In his house. Something to thank his parents for all they had done, a source of stability and warmth for his home. A place for them to be protected and to live in luxury.

Feelings he hadn't counted on, hadn't wanted from her. But

it wasn't the end of everything. He could keep her. He could make her happy. And he could do it without endangering her.

Without exposing himself.

It was wrong to want this. But he did.

He turned and walked back into the bedroom, looked at Paige curled up in bed. He slipped beneath the covers with her and gathered her close, pressing a kiss to her hair.

This could work. He would make it work. Tomorrow, when they were back home, he would tell her he wanted her to stay with him. And she would.

She had to.

CHAPTER FOURTEEN

PAIGE was overjoyed to be reunited with Ana, who had grown spoiled overnight in the company of the people who now considered themselves her grandparents. Her heart ached at the thought of what their deception was doing. Over the people it could hurt.

She hadn't counted on this. On how far it would spread. No, she hadn't thought at all. And now it had all become one big emotional tangle. Don and Mary Colson loved Ana, and she loved them. Ana loved Dante. Paige loved Dante and she had been foolish enough to tell him so.

And he hadn't said a thing back. Hadn't said a thing about it since, not even in denial of it, or rejection of it.

With his parents around, she hadn't really thought he would. But once they were gone and a very cranky Ana who was coming off being treated like her Royal Highness the Grand Duchess had been put down for her nap, she'd expected something.

Instead, Dante had retreated to the office. Really, it was Tuesday and they both could have gone in, but she'd felt sulky over his behavior, and reluctant to leave Ana, and he hadn't pressed.

Paige put the finishing touches on her sketch and looked out at the ocean. She had another window designed for Christmas, and with only one more main display to concern herself with, she was running well ahead of deadline.

Dante's seaside house was certainly good for inspiration.

Even if the man himself was turning her into a quivering ball of nerves.

She set her sketchbook down on the table and stood, stretching her arms up over her head, then shaking her hands out, trying to get rid of some of the adrenaline that was running through her.

Thinking about Dante had that effect on her. Remembering being in bed with him did that to her. Most especially, remembering that she'd told him she loved him had that effect on her.

She took a deep breath of the ocean air and put her hand on her stomach. Dante's parents, their feelings, were just a part of the unintended side effects of this whole thing. It was still possible that she was pregnant.

The idea had panicked her at first. The thought of caring for two babies. Of what it might do to the adoption. Now... now she felt like she could do it. Like no matter what happened, it was within her power to handle it.

Because she wasn't the same person she had been. Or rather, she didn't see herself the way her family, or the people back in her hometown had anymore. She wasn't deficient. She had everything in her that she needed to succeed. Most importantly, she knew just how much power love had. How it had changed her. With Ana, and now with Dante.

Another baby would mean more love. And no matter how difficult it might be to manage everything, she couldn't regret that.

She turned and walked back into the house, and nearly ran into Dante, who was walking through the living room with long, purposeful strides.

"You're back."

"Yes," he said. "I am."

"It's before five, so it surprised me."

"There was pressing business for me to take care of here."

"What...what's that?" she asked, sure she didn't want to know. Because she was sure she already knew. It had something to do with the I Love You incident and while she had wanted to talk to him about it, she found that, as she was faced with it, she was changing her mind.

"I've been thinking. The coverage of the wedding in the media has been very positive."

She grimaced. "Yeah, I hadn't really looked at it." Frankly, she hadn't wanted to see pictures of the moment she'd realized she was in love with the world's most impossible man.

"I had Trevor send me the highlights. But, as I thought, the wedding, the relationship in general, has had a very positive effect on my image."

"Well, that's nice." This was about as far from feelings as it got, and she found she was more annoyed than relieved.

"There is the possibility you're pregnant."

"I'll know soon-ish," she said.

"Also," he said, pressing on as if she hadn't spoken, "it didn't escape my notice how quickly Don and Mary took to Ana. And how quickly she took to them."

Her stomach fell. "Oh. Yeah, I feel bad about that."

"Why? There's no reason to. If anything, it confirms what I already suspected we should do."

"And what's that?" she asked, not sure she was going to like the answer. Afraid she might love it.

"I think this should be a permanent arrangement."

She did love it. A rush of joy, of complete and utter joy, filled her. "Really?"

"It seems the best thing to do, all things considered."

"Yes," she said, walking to him and throwing her arms around his neck. "Yes." Her mind went blank of everything, everything but the moment. Everything but him.

He pulled her in tightly, kissing her lips, his hands roaming over her curves. They kissed as they went up the stairs before Dante swung her up into his arms, holding her to his chest, his mouth devouring hers as he set her on the bed, stripping his clothes and hers as quickly as possible.

* * *

In the aftermath, she lay there replete, the room spinning, her heart pounding. She rolled over, ready to pull Dante into her arms, but he was already up and getting dressed, his expression tight, shuttered.

"I think we've proven that there are even more reasons for us to stay together," he said, as he tugged his pants on, his tone conversational. "The chemistry between us is incredible."

"The chemistry?" she said, feeling thick and fuzzy from her release still. Chemistry didn't sound right, though. It sounded like nothing more than a base, chemical reaction and yet she felt like there was so much more between them. There was for her, at least.

"It's the best sex I've ever had."

She felt struck by that comment. So bald and so basic. At any other time, she might have found it sexy to hear him say that, felt complimented. But when she'd offered love twelve hours before, and this was her gift in return, no, it didn't feel so good.

"And is that...all?" she asked.

"There's nothing more, Paige. Nothing else that matters."

"Dante..."

"Now that we've settled things, I do have more work to do." He tugged his shirt on and buttoned it with deft, steady fingers. He slicked his hair back with his hand and it was like nothing had just happened between them. As if a storm hadn't just blown through the room, blown through them.

He turned and walked out of the room, closing the door firmly behind him. Paige pulled her knees up to her chest and sat there, stunned. She felt...sad. Drained. Used.

She let the feeling wash over her, wash through her. But only for a moment.

Then she remembered the look in his eyes. That awful blank look that she knew so well. Dante was running scared. Trying to have the basest arrangement with her without giving anything of himself. Only his money, his body.

But she wouldn't accept that. The old Paige would have. She wouldn't have tried for more.

But this Paige, this woman who was, in part of Dante's making, was going to try for everything. All she needed was a plan.

Dante couldn't concentrate on his work. He could concentrate on nothing. He had left work at three in the afternoon, come home and had passionate, intense… It was sex and yet at the same time, something more, with a woman who seemed determined to break him open with a battering ram.

And she was close. Too close.

Three hours on and his body still burned. His chest aching like there was a hole in it.

"Dante."

He turned and his heart nearly stopped. Paige was standing there, a chiffon gown that had no substance at all wound around her curves, the light behind her showing the silhouette of her body beneath the gown.

"What are you doing?" he asked, his throat tightening, threatening to choke him.

"I'm here to talk."

"You don't look like you're here to talk," he said.

"But I am. I'm here to lay it out for you, as clear and honest as I can."

"Lay what out?"

"Everything. What I feel. What I feel for you. I'm not going to do it while I'm half-asleep, while you can pretend you didn't hear. I'm going to tell you now, to your face."

She crossed the threshold of his office and came to stand in front of his chair, her blue eyes bright, determined. She cupped his face, her eyes never leaving his as she leaned in and pressed a kiss to his forehead.

"I love you," she whispered. She kissed his cheek. "I love you." Then his lips, the touch feather-soft and perfect. "I love you."

He gritted his teeth, trying to fight against the pain, the need, that was building in his chest, threatening to over-whelm him, to consume him completely. "I'm glad, Paige. If that makes you happy, then I'm glad."

"Is that all?" she asked, searching his face, demanding honesty.

He gritted his teeth and looked away. "It's all I have to give."

"You're a liar, Dante."

Anger flooded through him, unreasonable and hot. "I'm a what?"

"A liar. And not just about this. Your entire life is a lie. Your whole existence."

He pushed up from his chair and she leaped backward, her eyes wide with shock. "Of course," he snarled, battling against the pain in his chest. "How could I forget? I'm the Italian bastard, adopted by a respectable family. The one who doesn't belong. Of course my existence is a lie. I have spent years pretending to be civilized, pretending to be a man of honor, when we both know I am not. I don't share their blood," he said, speaking of his parents. "I have the blood of a killer in me. The blood of a low-class, violent coward who abused women. Killed them. That's who I am...of course this is a lie," he said, sweeping his hand around the well-ordered, perfect room. The lie he had built for himself.

He stared her down, stared into her wide eyes, waiting for the fear to win. Waiting for her to realize that what he said was true. That he wasn't the man she thought he was. That he wasn't the man he pretended to be. That beneath his armor, was a darkness that no one would ever want to touch.

"No," she said, shaking her head. "You idiot. You think I don't know that's what you think of yourself? You think I buy what the press writes? What you show everyone? Don't forget I'm the one who dragged you out of that cold shower. I'm the one who warmed you with her own body, so don't try to scare me now with the same lie you tell yourself every day.

Because this is the lie, Dante Romani. That you're broken. That you can't love or be loved. Look around you…people love you. Because you're worthy of it. Don and Mary love you. Ana loves you. I love you. And you won't let us. Because you're too damn afraid."

"Hell, yes, I'm afraid," he growled, feeling the walls he'd erected around his heart crumbling. "I am half of that man, Paige. Do you know what that means? Passion is poison for me. It could be."

"It's not true."

"You think it's not true. Why? Because you love me? *She* loved him, Paige." He shouted the words, desperate to make her understand, to make her believe him. "That's why she didn't leave. She loved him…she thought he could be different. That he could change. Don't you understand? Love doesn't fix anything. It hides flaws. Makes people blind to them. But love is not all brightness and sunshine. It can't heal a damned thing." His voice broke, the memories of his mother flooding his mind. "It has a dark side. Everything does."

She shook her head. "Only if you choose to dwell in the dark. He made a choice, Dante. You can't blame love for that. That wasn't love."

"Passion then. Emotion. A lack of control. I won't let myself do that. Do you see this?" he asked, sweeping his arm across his office. "Order. Control. That's who I am. It's what I've made myself. What I've trained myself to be. So that I will never hurt someone like that. So that I will never become that man."

"So that you'll never be hurt," she said, her voice soft.

"That, too," he said, everything in him feeling exposed now. Raw.

"This isn't real," she said, looking around the room. "It's just stuff. It's just the outside. It doesn't fix who you are."

He laughed, the sound divorced from humor. "Nothing can, I'm afraid. All I can do is keep hiding who I am. Keep it locked up."

She bit her lip and shook her head. "You're a good man, Dante. I don't know why you don't know it. Why you don't believe it. Look what you've done for me. For Ana. You keep almost every bit of yourself locked up tight and you make me work to reach it, but when I do, that's when I know."

"When you know what?" he asked, his lungs frozen, incapable of drawing breath.

"When I know that I love you. And not just that, but why. Because you are so strong. And so broken. And yet, in spite of everything you've been through, you've grown up to be a good man. A man who puts the needs of others before himself. A man who is capable of great love, if only he would let himself feel it."

He shook his head. "That's not me, Paige. I'm sorry you're confused about that."

"You love me," she said.

Something inside of him broke completely, opening up a flood of emotion, of need so strong he wasn't sure he could withstand the onslaught. But he stood still, composing his face into a mask, doing what he had to do.

"No."

She shook her head. "I don't believe that."

"Then you have fooled yourself."

A tear spilled down her cheek, then another, each track of moisture a stab in his chest, a drop of his own blood shed inside, bleeding him dry. She shook her head. "No, Dante. Stop now. How long will you punish yourself for sins your father committed?"

"Love only means one thing to me, Paige. It is rage, and loss and grief so deep it consumes everything in its path. It puts you on your knees, steals your breath with the pain that it causes."

"That isn't love, Dante. That's evil. It was evil that tore love from you, that made your father do what he did. There was no love in it."

"Then it's the potential for evil I see in myself. Thank you for making it clear."

"You say you're half of your father like that makes everything certain. Like you aren't half of your mother. Don't forget that. Don't forget she gave you life, and that she would want you to live it fully. And don't forget what Don and Mary gave you, not through genetics, but what they taught you. You're bigger than one man, bigger than one event."

"And you speak like you have anything more than frivolous thoughts in your head," he growled, hating the insult, hating the words even as they left his lips. He was a coward. And in that moment, he knew it. Knew he was using anger to make her leave so he wouldn't have to listen to her anymore.

Because she was too close to tearing the veil away. To exposing him, not just to her, but to himself, for the first time.

"Out," he said. "Get out."

She stood for a moment, her blue eyes fixed on his, windows into her soul. Her pain, her sadness, worst of all, her love. For him. Love he didn't deserve. Couldn't accept.

"Get out, Paige. I don't want you here. I don't want you." The last words were torn from him, taking a piece of his soul with them. A lie he had to tell. A lie he hated.

She bit her bottom lip and nodded, then turned and walked out of the room, closing the door behind her. He didn't want to follow her. He didn't want to watch her walk out of the house, drive away. Out of his life. He would deserve it. He should want it.

But he didn't. He so desperately didn't. He wanted to cling to her words. To tell her that she was right. To will himself to believe it no matter what. So he could have her. So he could have Ana.

He looked around his desk, it was well-ordered. So perfect. And for the first time, he realized that everything around him was a lie. He was broken. Disheveled. Destroyed. And no amount of cleaning his surroundings would fix it.

He put his hand on his desk, on top of a mug that was

placed at a right angle, in the exact spot it needed to be for him to reach it with ease when he was seated. He picked it up by the handle and looked at it, felt the weight of it in his hand.

And he looked back down at the surface of his desk. A place for everything, everything in its place. And he hated it.

He growled and hurled the mug at the wall, splintering it into a hundred pieces. He braced himself on the desk, then he pushed everything to the floor.

His pencil holder. Stapler. The lamp. The damn zen garden that was supposed to make him feel calm. A stack of papers. Until his office was littered with the kind of destruction that mirrored the man he was within.

Piece by piece, he exposed himself. Tore away the walls. Tore away the facade until he had to look at it. Until he had to look at himself.

Pain tore at his chest. For once, he didn't have to strike out to cause physical agony as punishment. It was all in him, burning him alive from the inside out. He dropped to his knees, leaned forward, his forehead and forearms touching the floor.

She was right. He was a liar. He was scared, of himself. But not only of that, of caring and losing again. So much so, he had spent his life training himself never to care, on the excuse that he was protecting everyone from himself.

When he was really protecting himself from everyone else. Still a scared child, hiding behind a sofa, waiting, waiting for the monster to find him. A monster from outside, or a monster inside of himself.

He had believed, wholly, that he had banished his every emotion. But it was a lie, too. He hadn't. He had simply embraced fear and allowed it to dictate everything he did. Who he was.

For a brief moment in time, he'd had love in this house. A woman who loved him. A child who trusted him completely.

And he had thrown it away. The final punishment for his sins. The ultimate penance. He had fallen in love. The thing he had sworn he must never do. And he had done it. So he had pushed her away, pushed them away.

And now he was reduced to nothing. Raw and bleeding, all of his protection gone. All of his defenses, his ways of dealing, exposed for the flimsy nothings they were. He could do nothing. Nothing but lie there and embrace the pain, the love, the misery, the loss. Not just for Paige, not just for Ana, but for every moment in his life.

The walls he'd built to protect himself burned to nothing, reduced to ash before his eyes. He was not the man he pretended to be. He was not the man the media thought he was. And he let himself hope, for a moment, that he was the man that Paige saw. A man worthy of her love, worthy of Ana's admiration. Worthy of the Colsons' adoption.

For a long time he lay there, stripped of his protection. Of everything. Anguish washing over him, beating against him.

Finally, he stood, his hands shaking, and dialed his mother and father's phone number.

"Dante?" His mother answered on the second ring.

"Why did you adopt me?" he asked. He had never asked. He had always feared the answer. Had always feared that the media was right. And over the years, he had simply started to assume they were.

More than that, he was afraid of loving again. Of caring and losing. But that fear had carried him nowhere. That fear had nothing for him. Had given him nothing.

"Because," she said, her tone simple, matter-of-fact, "we fell in love with you the moment we saw you. An angry teenage boy with so much potential, in so much need. We knew you were our son. The one we'd been waiting for."

"I wasn't ready to hear that," he said, swallowing hard, holding the phone tight to his ear. "Until now."

"I know," she whispered.

He closed his eyes and released his hold on fear. "I love you," he said.

CHAPTER FIFTEEN

PAIGE felt like she was dying. Ana hadn't slept the whole night. She couldn't really blame her. She was in her little bassinet, rather than her crib, and crammed back into Paige's old room, in her old apartment. As a result, Paige hadn't slept, either.

She'd thought coming back to her little apartment would give her some clarity. Make her feel more...more like Dante and everything else had never happened. But it hadn't helped. She was too different. Too changed from her time with him. There was no way to even pretend it hadn't happened.

Now she was sitting at her desk, after having weathered a sea of congratulations from the other employees on her way into the office, feeling like death and having just spent the night away from her new husband, who was probably never going to speak to her again.

She would have to go back to Dante's house, she knew that. But one night couldn't have hurt. No one would find out. It would hardly compromise the adoption. And she needed space. Needed to not be sharing the same air as Dante.

She knew that he'd lashed out because she'd challenged him. Because he was frightened. She knew it down in her soul. But just because she was right, didn't mean he would change his mind. Didn't mean he would decide to change a lifetime of thinking and feeling a certain way. Didn't mean he even wanted to.

Maybe she was wrong about him loving her—that could be true. He loved Ana, though. She could see that. And she knew, given the chance, that he would be an amazing father. The kind of man who offered support and love to his children.

She'd known it the moment she'd seen him there, singing Ana his lullaby. She knew that had cost him, and that Ana's needs had transcended his grief. She'd known in that moment that he was a man capable of great love. And that he'd let fear cripple him.

Stupid man. Stupid, fantastic, lovely man.

"Mrs. Romani?"

It took Paige a moment to realize she was being addressed, even though she was in her office. She looked up and saw a young man standing at the door, a newspaper in his hand.

"Yes?"

"I'm supposed to deliver this to you." He came in and set the paper on her desk.

"Oh…" She looked down at her desk, frowning. "Oh…I… thank you…" She looked up and the man was gone.

She picked up the paper and started to turn each page, looking for…she didn't know what. Had someone wanted her to see pictures of the wedding? She flipped to the style section, and the headline stopped her cold.

She put her hand over her mouth, a sob climbing her throat. She picked up the paper, gathered it close to her chest, stood and ran out of her office.

"Explain this," Paige said, throwing the newspaper onto Dante's desk, a tear rolling down her cheek. She was shaking. Everywhere.

Dante looked up at her, his eyes haunted, the veil well and truly dropped. There was no armor covering up his emotions, nothing protecting him. He was as bare and vulnerable as she was.

"I told the truth," he said, his voice rough. "For the first time in so long, I told the truth."

She read the headline out loud. "Recently Wed Dante Romani Proclaims: I Love My Wife."

"It's true," he said.

Another tear slid down her cheek and she looked down at the paper, reading out loud.

"It was speculated only a few weeks ago, about whether or not Ms. Harper could reform ice-cold Dante Romani, and today he has confirmed that, indeed she has. 'I love my wife,' Romani says, 'and love changes you.'"

She looked back up at him. "This is a fluff piece," she said, sniffling. "No hard-hitting journalism, just a page of you talking about h-how much you love me, and your parents. And Ana."

"I admit that maybe doing it in a public forum wasn't the best thing but...all things considered..."

"Turnabout's fair play."

"Yes," he said. "Yes, it is. But this doesn't replace what I need to say to you now. I love you."

Paige's heart expanded in her chest, more tears falling. "Dante, you're ruining my makeup."

"And you completely destroyed the way I saw myself, and life, so I'd say it's a fair trade." He stood and walked around his desk, his eyes intent on hers. "You were right, Paige. I lied to myself. Because I was afraid. Of everything. Part of me was locked up tight, and I never intended on letting it out. Not ever. But you've shown me, consistently, that the reward for bravery is worth the risk. You've been so brave, so much braver than I. You took a risk to protect Ana... You took a risk in confessing your love to me. You put yourself out there time and again and opened yourself up to rejection when you didn't have to do that. And I was too cowardly to do the same."

Paige tried to swallow past the lump in her throat. "We've

had different life experiences, Dante. I can't even imagine what you went through. What that does to someone."

"It changes you," he said, his eyes filled with pain. "There's no way around that. But what you said…it's very true. And I can't let my fear of a man so far in my past be more important than the woman here in my present, and my future. You were right. People do love me, and I have been afraid to accept it. To look for it. To see it. Because I didn't want pain or grief to touch me ever again. And because of that, I've been living a cold life. I thought that by keeping everything well-ordered around me, that by accumulating more things, more success, I would somehow change from who I was into who I needed to be. But none of it mattered. None of it was real. None of it changed me. It just let me hide. From myself. From everyone. Everyone except you. You dragged me into the light. And I've learned something, Paige."

"What's that?" she asked.

"Light is stronger. I used to think that the two of them were different sides of the same coin. That with one, always came the other. That way of thinking…it helped me reason out what had happened when I was kid. It helped me find a way to believe that by behaving a certain way, I could control things. And now I've realized two things, the first being that I can't control everything. And the second is that light casts out darkness. When you shine it bright, it fills every corner, and it eradicates anything dark. There is nowhere for it to hide. That's what you've done for me. You shone a light on my soul, and now I'm filled with it. With your love."

She threw her arms around his neck and kissed him hard on the mouth. "I love you so much."

"I love you, too, Paige. I am so thankful for everything you are, because it's everything I needed. You are perfect in every way."

"Even when I get glitter on you?"

"Even then. Maybe especially then. Because I love that you come with color, and paint, and glitter."

"And a baby?"

"Most especially a baby. I want to be your husband," he said, "forever. And I also want to be Ana's father. Her real father. I never let myself realize just how much this is true, but I have a wonderful example of what a father should be in Don Colson. And I want to be that for Ana. I want to guide her, support her and love her. I'm afraid I'll mess it up, but I want to try."

"And if she wants to be an artist slash window dresser like her mother?"

"She's welcome to it. I'll build her an art studio."

"What about if she wants to be a CEO like her father?"

"She could do that, too. She can do anything."

"I think she can, too," Paige said, happiness filling her, suffusing her.

"And one of the most important things I hope to teach her, is through example," he said, his voice getting rough. "I hope to show her what love looks like, every day. By loving her as a father should love a daughter. And I hope to show her the kind of love that should exist between a husband and wife, by loving her mother, every day, as long as we both shall live."

EPILOGUE

Ana started crawling the day the adoption was finalized.

"She's really moving now," Paige said.

Dante watched Ana rock back and forth on her hands and knees before moving forward again, heading straight for the coffee table. He scooped her up into his arms, keeping her from certain disaster. "You have to watch your head, *stellina*," he said.

Ana had most definitely become his little star, not just because she was one of the two people at the center of his universe, but because she had healed so much pain in him.

He had vowed to teach Ana what love was, and yet, he found she was the one who taught him. Every day.

"Before you know it, she'll be dating," Paige said, giving him a mischievous smile.

He frowned. "No. I'm not thinking that far ahead."

"Why? Are you afraid some handsome Italian is going to come and sweep her off her feet?"

"Yes," he said.

Paige laughed. "You do have to watch those Italians. I should know. I'm a terminal case for the one I married."

She looped her arms around both him and Ana and kissed him on the cheek.

"So you don't regret it?" he asked, knowing she didn't, but liking to hear it anyway.

"Nope. Not one bit. There is one thing that will be hard to explain to Ana, though."

"What's that? Why you and I disappear behind closed bedroom doors for hours on end?"

She laughed. "Uh, I don't plan on explaining that. But that isn't what I meant."

"What then?"

"It'll be hard to explain to her why telling a lie led to the best thing that ever could have happened to me."

* * * * *

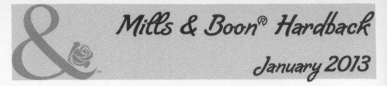

Mills & Boon® Hardback

January 2013

ROMANCE

MEDICAL

Mills & Boon® Large Print

January 2013

ROMANCE

HISTORICAL

MEDICAL

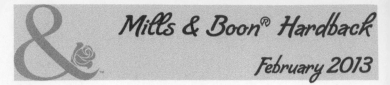

Mills & Boon® Hardback

February 2013

ROMANCE

MEDICAL

0113 GEN STD HB

ROMANCE

Banished to the Harem	Carol Marinelli
Not Just the Greek's Wife	Lucy Monroe
A Delicious Deception	Elizabeth Power
Painted the Other Woman	Julia James
Taming the Brooding Cattleman	Marion Lennox
The Rancher's Unexpected Family	Myrna Mackenzie
Nanny for the Millionaire's Twins	Susan Meier
Truth-Or-Date.com	Nina Harrington
A Game of Vows	Maisey Yates
A Devil in Disguise	Caitlin Crews
Revelations of the Night Before	Lynn Raye Harris

HISTORICAL

Two Wrongs Make a Marriage	Christine Merrill
How to Ruin a Reputation	Bronwyn Scott
When Marrying a Duke...	Helen Dickson
No Occupation for a Lady	Gail Whitiker
Tarnished Rose of the Court	Amanda McCabe

MEDICAL

Sydney Harbour Hospital: Ava's Re-Awakening	Carol Marinelli
How To Mend A Broken Heart	Amy Andrews
Falling for Dr Fearless	Lucy Clark
The Nurse He Shouldn't Notice	Susan Carlisle
Every Boy's Dream Dad	Sue MacKay
Return of the Rebel Surgeon	Connie Cox